PETER'S MOONLIGHT PHOTOGRAPHY

AND OTHER STORIES

by Dina Rabadi

ACKNOWLEDGEMENTS

I want to thank a number of people who have supported, loved and encouraged me. My mother and father, Dana Rabadi and Suleiman Rabadi. My siblings and their partners: Abdo, Andrea, Linda, Jeremy, Alan, Kristen. Also, Dan and Jody Daunhauer. My grandmother: Božena Krejcarová. My Czech aunt, Ivana Zajičková and cousin: Lenka Zajičková. Someone very special to me: Neri Orellana. My mentors, Ann Mladinov, Vincent Schodolski, Mark Watson and the late Farouk Mustafa. My colleagues and friends: Abel Alves, Josef Zak, David Evanier, Anne Sippel, Imrana Khera, Noha Aboulmagd Forster, Steve and Sherri Nelson, Mahima Joishy, Nicki Harada, Wanda McGill, Laura McGlone Allen, Jack and Laura Doyle, Marre Violante, and the late Jeff Leigh. Special thanks to Jennifer Mikulina for her legal counsel and kindness, thank you to Robert Bernstein, CPA as well as Marci Rolnik and Lawyers for the Creative Arts. Thank you Eric Christensen, Kady Dennell and Victoria Shapow for being part of this project. You are all so talented. I will always be grateful to my friend, Indrani de Silva, and her mother, Gail Scott, for encouraging me to become a writer that first year at Smith College.

FIRST EDITION 2015

Copyright © 2015 by Dina Rabadi

www.DinaRabadi.com

First published in 2015 in Chicago

ISBN: 978-09903003-0-4

"Silver Boxes" was first published in *Fiction*, "The Phone Call" in *Downstate Story Magazine* and "Watershots" (title later changed to "Water, Water Everywhere") in *The Armchair Aesthete*. The author wished to thank the editors of these publications for their support.

CONTENTS

Peter's Moonlight Photography

Talented Photographer
Needs Models
All Ages, All Sizes
Women Only
For Moonlight Photography
(Be Nymph-like)
Call Peter
818-365-8765

1

Peter knew he would be famous any day now. He wrote about it every night in his Ansel Adams limited edition sugar pine diary.

"I can feel it coming," he began, underlining "it" twice and putting "fame" in parentheses while shifting positions in his king-sized waterbed.

"Roland will give me a contract. I know he will this time. I dropped off the photos five months ago. Five months ago?" He counted backwards on his Frito-covered fingers as two waves carried him to the other side of his man-made ocean. He paused. *Nervous*, he thought to himself, as he blew a long, low note into his harmonica. "He wants to make me nervous because he figures every photography gallery in the country wants me."

He switched sides, then pens, then gave up altogether to focus on harmonica playing. He held the windowed silver box against his heart. If he hadn't been an artist, he would have been a musician, like B.B. King or Jimmy McGriff or Neil Young. Then "Boogie Chillin'" came on the small kitchen radio. *Or like John Lee Hooker*, he thought, putting the harmonica to his lips and blowing two nearly perfect notes.

◆ ◆ ◆

Peter was a short, skinny man in his early fifties with a butter-colored mustache and a thick head of hair the same color -- just like the Clairol coloring kit that he kept under his bed had recommended.

He had a handsome face -- clean, blue eyes, weathered, caramel-colored skin, and thick, pink lips the same color and texture as the ribeyes that he loved to grill on his George Foreman.

When he actually grilled outside, he wore a light gray Stetson hat that his dad had gotten him in Vegas and looked strikingly like the Marlboro man on the giant cigarette billboard ad next to his California house. Lots of people noticed.

"Wow," said three college kids last week, on their way to the Burbank cinema just past his house. "That's a great picture of you. Did you ask them to put that there?"

"No," Peter shouted, putting down *Art World at Your Fingertips* so that he could properly yell at them. "Do I look like I want to die of lung cancer?"

"Yes," they answered, and sped off.

"Damn kids," he said, as he took out his Marlboros from the pocket of his salmon-colored shirt.

He was much nicer to the ladies, although he lied to them about his age. The youngest he ever got away with was thirty-two till he slipped up and told the college girl that he walked with a limp because he got shot in the leg in Nam by "those damn rice-eaters."

11

"Nam?" she said. "As in Vietnam? One of those rice eaters was my grandmother."

"I had no idea," he said.

"She should have shot your other leg as well, you racist phony."

"Damn women," he huffed. "All they're good for is a lousy picture."

And Peter should know. He had over two hundred photos of women, most of them taken over the past five years, under moonlight. Big ones, little ones, fat ones, young ones, old ones, red heads, blondes, and brunettes.

He had been a self-declared artist for many years, until he took a series of classes at a nearby community college to make it official. "Fine Art Photographer," the diploma said. "Expires in two years," it continued in fine print, "if renewal course is not taken." But Peter's eyesight was bad and he missed that part. Still, it was a diploma, and since it was the only one he had, it meant something.

He hung the diploma next to his first photo, "Moonlight Madness, 1981," which he took of the full moon after drinking an entire bottle of vodka. He said he got the "madness" idea because his hands kept shaking and he kept seeing two or three moons when he snapped the picture. He liked the results so much that for the next two years, he only took pictures of the moon, from different perspectives. From his car window, his rooftop, his front lawn, his back lawn, and once, he said most proudly, in the eyes of his ex-wife as she lay on her back after they had made love in the driveway. That picture he swore no one would see.

That combination of flesh and moonlight inspired him to use moonlight as his only source of light and women as his only subjects. After his divorce, it became much easier to do.

His small house had gone to hell since his wife had left him, the furniture yellowing and crumbling, the carpet stained and wearing away, even the mail was neglected, growing uncontrollably in the corner under the slot where it fell into the house. Peter didn't care. All he cared about was his art. He knew he hadn't been much of a husband, a housekeeper, a lover, or a musician. But his art, that was something he was good at. It was only a matter of time before someone else noticed.

So he shoved two couches out of the living room, ripped out the carpeting, installed hard wood, put track lighting along the walls, and hung up four of his favorite moonlight photos right next to each other: Sherry, Cindy, Tonya, and Terry.

The photos were huge, six feet by eight feet, each photo taking up half a wall. But most startling were the women: naked, hanging from trees and climbing out of bushes in the most ridiculous positions. It was easy to see that Peter had intended the women to seem dreamlike, their pale flesh translucent under the moonlight, glimpses of hands, feet and hair from the branches, shiny eyes between leaves. "Nymph-like" was more precise, that's how he had described it in his ad:

Talented Photographer
Needs Nude Models
All Ages, All Sizes
Women Only

For Moonlight Photography
(Be Nymph-like)
Call Peter
818-365-8765

"The moon," he told the women who responded to his ad. "I want to photograph you being one with the moon." Most of them would hang up on him at this point, especially since he offered the moon but no money. But some were interested, convinced or perhaps seduced by his husky voice and the nymph motif he promised.

PETER'S MOONLIGHT PHOTOGRAPHY

"Sherry"
L'été 1984
color lithograph
6' x 8'

15

2

Sherry had come across Peter's ad while looking for an apartment in Santa Monica. She would be a sophomore at Wellesley in the fall, but for now had a summer internship in southern California researching environmental law.

She had never responded to an ad for models before. She didn't think she was model material. She was short (5'1), meaty in places (they used to call her "stump" in high school), and self-conscious about her left eye (partially crossed).

She was grateful for having a body that was functional (except for her left eye), but like most average-looking people who have accepted their averageness, she occasion-ally thought about the alternative—having the kind of beauty that gets exalted in the streets, in bars, on the dance floor, on magazine covers.

She thought modeling for Peter would satisfy this need to be exalted without compromising her feminist beliefs. This was fine art—not *Penthouse*. She would help Peter with his mission of self-expression. She could think of it as community service. And to be thought of as the most beautiful woman/nymph in the world for even one night would be magical.

So she called Peter and went over to his house that same night for an interview. He liked her look right away: light-skinned (to pick up the moonlight), sturdy (she would have to climb trees), with long red hair (his favorite color).

The next weekend they packed up his red Chevy, some beef jerky, and his harmonica, and headed north towards the citrus groves of Santa Clara Valley. A few hours later, darkness fell and Peter pulled over. He led Sherry by the hand to a grassy area by the first of a long line of lemon trees under the full moon.

"Okay," he said. "Drop your clothes."

"I was thinking," she said, "that maybe I should keep some on. Be more subtle. You could wrap a white sheet around me, sort of cloud-like, with my hair up like this…" she started to show him.

"No," he said. "I want nymph-like, not cloud-like. No clothes."

She zipped up her jacket and stared at him.

"Nymphs are always naked," he pleaded. "See?" He pulled out a German fine art catalogue from one of his equipment bags. "Turn to page 23."

She did, and sure enough, there was a section on nymphs and they were all naked.

"Fine," she said. And stripped.

"Now get in the tree. Quickly. I'm losing light."

"I'm not getting in the tree," she said. "I'll look ridiculous."

"Look, Sherry," he said sternly. "I have a vision. A beautiful vision that I would like you to be a part of. This isn't going to work if you don't trust me. Now I've done this with other women, of course none of them as beautiful as you, but they trusted me. Nymphs,are not only naked, but reside in trees, bushes, and mountains." Then he bent down to get his German art catalogue again.

"Okay, I believe you. Just hurry up. It's cold out here."

So Peter snapped several pictures of her in the tree, next to the tree, and on the grass. She was nervous at first, but relaxed when she realized he wasn't trying to take advantage of her. Her poses weren't obscene. And he never touched her. He was sincere about his vision. He wanted to be the best moonlight photographer in the country.

She knew he never would be. She had seen his pictures. But she also knew that she was not beautiful. Yet here, in the moonlight, anything seemed possible.

"Beautiful," he said, over and over again. "Exquisite. Yes. Arch a little more. You're my best subject yet." She blushed, then laughed and threw her head back against the lemon tree and let the moonlight fall on her face. She held still for a moment, looking up at purple sky, then she turned and looked directly into the camera. He caught it. That was the first one he framed.

"Cindy"
L'automne 1984
color lithograph
6' x 8'

3

Cindy liked to keep up with the celebrity reports. This new actress was dating so-and-so. This new actor was now behind bars. This so-and-so actress was filming in Africa. This so-so director was upset about it. She plucked them from the magazine stand like autumn grapes -- holding them up to the light, to her lips, to her heart, till the Chinese checkout girl would ask her if everything was alright.

"Yep," she would answer. "I'll buy these and ten more boxes of soap."

Cindy was forty and ran a laundromat on Wilshire Blvd. next to an Asian-American grocery store and a Croatian bookstore. She was neither Asian nor Croatian but part Irish, part English, and part Turkish. She was not sure where the Turkish part came from. Her father had been the first two parts, her mother the same. It was only later, when she had gotten older that her mother had told her about the summer she had spent in Turkey while her father had been stationed there with the military.

"A girl also craves adventure," her mother confessed. "And not always of the geographic kind."

She had not been angry with her mother. Instead, from then on, she supported her biological father's country by buying only Turkish cotton and Turkish coffee. While she sometimes felt the urge to seek him out, it never overcame her completely. Surrounded by Turkish sheets and holding a cup of Turkish coffee, she caught sight of her dark eyes in her bedroom mirror and thought, "What for? He is already with me."

◆ ◆ ◆

Three new issues of *Paper Mouth* were on the stand. Each cover featured the perspective of one of three sparring lovers. Which one was she rooting for? She bought all three. Below them were several fashion magazines, young women were on the covers of all of them, breasts bulging, pupils dilating, lips reddening. She reached to grab them, accidentally dropping one to the ground. She bent down to pick it up, and while lifting it up, compared the model's legs, breasts, and exotic face to her own.

"At least I have my Turkish eyes," she told herself. But it did not make her feel any better.

She put the magazine back as well as the three celebrity issues. She left the soap on the counter.

◆ ◆ ◆

For a week she did not go into the store to buy more soap or magazines. Instead she stayed inside her apartment which was attached to the laundromat and swished around in the tub as the clothes swished around outside. She put another handful of detergent into the water. Her old celebrity magazines lay on the floor.

21

"Dolls," she cried out loud. "Nothing but celebrity dolls we hold up, then crash together."

Then she remembered the models. Oh, the models were different. They were elevated, revered, held up at another level. Goddesses on earth-- made sacred, made divine. She looked at her own thighs through the turquoise bubbles then closed her eyes.

By the time she got done with her bath, she was quite red and had developed a rash. She wrapped a towel around herself and went out to check on the store. It was 9:50 p.m., almost time to close. Most of her customers were gone except for an elderly man who was washing his whites.

"My cycle is almost done," he shouted.

"No problem," she responded.

Even an elderly man did not seem excited at the sight of her in a towel. She turned away from him and began to collect the clothes that had been left behind.

As she picked up a red sweater, a flier fell out--

Talented Photographer
Needs Nude Models
All Ages, All Sizes
Women Only
For Moonlight Photography
(Be Nymph-like)
Call Peter
818-365-8765

She went to get the phone.

◆ ◆ ◆

"Just like Ansel," she said to Peter as they headed to Yosemite in his Chevy truck.

"I'm different than Ansel."

"But didn't he also shoot Yosemite?"

"Yosemite is a big place."

"I've never been there."

"Just wait," he said, picking up his harmonica and playing a few notes. "Just wait."

A few hours later they had entered the park. It was night time by then but the bare granite domes and other rock formations were visible in the moonlight.

"God is present here," said Peter, looking up. "Though we stopped talking a while ago."

"There's Half Dome," she shouted. Scrambling across his knees.

He stopped the car so she could get a better look. He looked up too. It rose in a perfect half-moon high above the valley.

"Didn't Ansel shoot this?"

"He did but what has that go to do with me? I'm not Ansel. I'm just influenced by his work."

They got back into the truck and continued driving till they reached Bridal Veil Falls. He parked the car then walked with her through the woods till they got to the site.

"Didn't Ansel shoot this too?" She asked as she spotted the waterfall behind him.

He didn't say anything. He began to set up his tripod.

He had wanted to photograph her in the trees, in a barren part that showed some of the waterfall behind her. He looked around for a good spot.

"What about the bears?" she asked.

"They won't hurt you," he said. "Don't you have your bear bells on?"

She did. She was naked otherwise but around each big toe was a bear bell.

"What if they don't work? Then what?"

"Fight."

"I thought I was supposed to play dead."

"You fight black bears and play dead with the brown ones."

"But it's dark out here, how will I be able to tell the difference?"

"Do some of both. Now get in the tree."

"Which tree?"

"The black oak behind you."

"But that's where the noise is coming from."

"Do you want me to photograph you or not?"

She paused to think about it. The waterfall seemed to get louder the longer she waited. As she was about to turn around to find out why, moonlight shot through the trees and illuminated her thighs. She looked down. They looked different. They looked smooth and strong and elegant, like the black oak beside her. Like the rest of the trees that surrounded her. Like the granite that rose above her. A mist fell upon her. It lit up too. Her skin became like chiffon. Though none of the moonlight settled in her eyes, for the first time in her life, she also felt that the rest of her was beautiful.

"Ready," she said.

He took the picture. That was the second one he framed.

"Tonya"
L'hiver 1985
color lithograph
6' x 8'

4

Peter and Tonya headed out to the desert.

"I thought this was going to be a winter shot?"

"It is winter."

"But where's the snow?"

"It's Los Angeles."

"I know, but we could have gone to Squaw Valley where there *is* snow and done a pretty shot with me in a handmade sweater... maybe a purple and gold one with bunny tracks going up and down my---"

"You're going to be naked."

"I didn't agree to that for sure."

"You saw the flier."

"That's true," she said. "I did see the flier. But if we go somewhere cold I'll have to wear a sweater. Even if it is somewhere hot I'll have to wear a sweater. Never mind about the gold and purple -- purple doesn't look good on black skin. But I really like those afghan-type sweaters with the frill along the bottom--"

"This isn't an ad for Sears. I am an artist. This is fine art."

"What's the difference?"

"Fine art has a vision."

"So does Sears."

"Their vision is to sell clothes and make money."

"So is yours."

"First of all there are absolutely no clothes in my shots whatsoever. Second of all, yes, I would like to make money, which separates me from the amateurs, but I have a vision that has nothing to do with money."

"What is it?"

"I can't tell you with words. That's why I'm an artist."

"You sound like Prince."

"I'm a photographer. You read the flier."

"Yeah. I read the flier. In fact I brought it with me." She took it out and looked at it again while he drove them south to Joshua National Park.

"Didn't U2 shoot the cover of their CD in Joshua Tree?"

"Yes, that's what inspired me."

"Isn't that copying?"

"No, it's called 'being inspired.'"

"It sounds like copying to me."

"Why do you care?"

"I have to deal with copyright issues all the time."

"Are you a patent lawyer?"

"No, I work at Kinko's. I have to make sure that the customers don't copy books without the written permission of the author or the artist. Do you realize how often that law gets violated?"

"Then you understand artists?"

"No, I just don't like cheaters. When I was a kid, I used to have all these ideas and kids in my class would always copy."

"How flattering."

"No, it's copying."

"It is a compliment to have people who want to copy your ideas. That means they are good ideas."

"I don't think Bono would be happy that you're copying."

"I'm not copying. I'm inspired by his work. Plus, I am not Bono, so I will have my own way of seeing the desert and you in the desert."

He stopped talking to concentrate on unwrapping his beef jerky. Tonya took out onion rings.

Dusk was falling and they were now at the start of the Mojave Desert. As they continued driving, teddy bear cholla and yuccas began to stud an otherwise sandy plain, completing what already looked like an abstract painting, a landscape that changed colors as the light changed -- pink, then purple, then burgundy. Eventually, they came to a stop and approached one of the biggest yuccas. It must have been forty feet tall – even taller, it seemed, with its elongated torso and outstretched, inquisitive arms.

"Is this a Joshua tree?"

"Yes," said Peter as he prepared his tripod.

Tonya looked back up at the tree.

"Why is it called a 'Joshua' tree?"

"When the Mormons were traveling through the desert in the 1800s they thought that the arms of the yuccas resembled the biblical prophet Joshua pointing the way to the Promised Land."

"Did it?"

"I don't know. I'm an atheist. Art is my promised land. Now get in the tree."

"How am I going to get in the tree? It's almost forty feet tall."

"You're right," he said. "Damn it. I should have brought a ladder."

"More like a helicopter."

They continued looking up at the tree.

"Okay, get undressed and we'll shoot you in the cholla instead."

"The bushes? You want to shoot me in the bushes? I bet the white women you shot were up in the trees, you racist!."

"Trust me. I have a vision."

He was standing in front of the yucca. His camera in his right hand, film he had been about to load in the other.

"Okay, okay."

She got behind a large rock beside the tree and changed. *Can't be more than forty degrees out here*, she thought, *and it's probably going to start snowing*. She put down her onion rings and looked up at the sky. No, no snow yet. She was now bare-chested.

She had not been bare-chested since she was nine. She used to love to run around with her brothers without her shirt on. But then, quickly, her breasts had grown. Grown and grown and grown and grown. As she got older, she had thought about getting surgery to reduce them. But she was too scared. Scared she would lose feeling there. She didn't understand how other women could risk that. So she wore sweaters. Lots of sweaters.

Living in Los Angeles complicated things. She would get so hot -- especially during the summer -- so she just tried to stay in places with air conditioning. That ruled out the beach. The beach -- oh, how she would love to be able to go to the beach and be like the men. She envied men and their freedom to take off their shirt. It must feel good to have air on your chest. Air on your chest. She began to laugh.

"What are you doing over there? Hurry up! I'm getting cold."

"You're getting cold? You have ten layers on. I'm the one bare-chested."

Bare-chested. Bare-chested. If it weren't for his flier she never would have done this. Nymph-like. Yes, she would like to be nymph-like. With her breasts and her body weight she was anything but nymph-like in daylight. She came out from behind the rock and crawled into the cholla on the other side. She was on her hands and knees, trying to figure out the best place to position her hands. Then she caught sight of the moon -- the glorious moon -- big and bold, white and wild, and thought, *so this is why wolves howl.*

"Great! Great!" yelled Peter. He began to take pictures.

The wind picked up. Blowing cold air on her. She did not mind. She lifted her hands off the ground, high above her head. She was bare-chested. It felt good. She was bare-chested. She felt good. She felt free. She felt beautiful. She was glad she had decided against the operation.

He snapped the picture. That was the third one he framed.

"Terry"
Le printemps 1985
color lithograph
6' x 8'

5

He decided to photograph Terry in Monument Valley. She was part Navaho and her height would compliment the spires. In fact, she could have been a spire. She must have been close to 6' 5".

"Utah?" she said, as she got in his truck. "I thought you were a California photographer."

"I am. But Americans are terrible at geography. They won't know the difference."

"But the Europeans aren't and they do most of the buying."

"Get in or I'm leaving you."

She laughed and shut the door.

◆ ◆ ◆

Terry was thirty-three and a mother of three, though she had never intended to be. She had meant to have a successful career as a pastry chef specializing in chocolate sculptures. She had gotten an entry-level position at a prestigious French restaurant. Then she had an affair with the bus boy. That was the first child. Then she got a job at an Austrian pastry shop and had an affair with the window cleaner. Child number two. And then an affair with… oh, it did not matter. She now had three children by three different fathers and was very far from making chocolate sculptures for a living.

She knew she had a "classic" problem. She had read about it in the self-help section of her local public library. She needed to have men find her attractive. What she really needed, she wanted to write in the book, was to find herself attractive so she wouldn't have to have men find her attractive. Better yet, to not have to worry about being attractive at all. Maybe then she could focus on making chocolate sculptures.

She envied the chefs that she knew who could. Most, she noticed, were men. How strange, she thought. Most of the people in the world who do the cooking are women, yet most of the top chefs are men. And look at them? Pudgy, short, bearded or unbearded, it did not matter. What mattered was that they could make beautiful chocolate sculptures.

She had made one, once, when she had been alone in her kitchen. The children were with her mother. There were no men that afternoon. It had been just her in the house making her chocolate sculpture in the nude. Yes, in the nude. She had wanted to get as close to her spirit as possible. For one hour, for one afternoon, it did not matter what she wore or what she looked like, but what she could create.

When it was finished, there were three waterfalls flowing down each side of a chocolate mountain and two humming-birds in the center. All she had to do was add one more wing to the second hummingbird. She was having a hard time getting to the torso of the bird, so she picked up the entire sculpture and tilted it towards her. But as she did so, she caught sight of herself in the silver platter. *I look like a butter knife*, she thought as she saw her reflection, tall and plain and angular. She dropped the wing, then the sculpture. The chocolate pieces shattered across the floor. She began to cry.

As she reached for a tissue, a piece of paper fell to the floor:

Talented Photographer
Needs Nude Models
All Ages, All Sizes
Women Only
For Moonlight Photography
(Be Nymph-like)
Call Peter
818-365-8765

◆ ◆ ◆

It was now late afternoon and Peter was now setting up his equipment at the foot of one of the spires. Terry was sitting in the curve of one of the nearby arches, her blonde hair pulled back. It was March in Monument Valley, near the small Indian town of Goudling, straddling the border of Arizona and Utah.

The ground was red, red like everything else in the area made of anything substantial -- mesas and buttes, sand hills and spires. She looked at the mesa closest to her -- round and flat-topped, curving down on the sides. It too was a dark red.

As evening fell, color became secondary. Shape took

precedence. Mesas, buttes, spires, and arches reached up from the ground like modern dancers. *What beautiful chocolate sculptures these would make*, she thought, as she admired the figures, reaching and receding in the evening light.

Peter looked up from the tripod he had just finished setting up. "Now we just have to wait for the moon."

She looked at him. She looked at him in *that* way.

"I'm an artist," he said quietly. "You're my model. It's a professional relationship."

She was hurt, but there was kindness in his eyes when said it. So she sat down next to him and also waited for the moon to appear.

When it did, she went behind the spire to change. She took her shirt off, then her socks and shoes. Just as she was about to take her pants off, she caught a glimpse of a rock formation off to her right that she had not noticed before. She put her shoes back on and walked closer to take a look. It looked like -- yes, a waterfall. And on the other side -- another waterfall. On the back, another. And on top -- yes, there were two hummingbirds -- with both of their wings! She began to clap, then went back to her changing spot. She put her shirt back on. Quickly, she came back around front to where Peter was waiting and grabbed his camera.

"What are you doing?" he asked. "What do you think you're doing?"

She ignored his question and ran back to the formation and began to take pictures -- of the waterfalls, of each of the hummingbirds. She kept going. Taking pictures of the spire she had changed by, of the arch she had sat in, of the other buttes and mesas and sand hills and spires that, up till now, she had only admired.

"What are you doing? What in the hell are you doing?" Peter said, yelling this time. He followed her.

She was now between two of the biggest rock formations -- giant spires that twirled up from the red earth, then bent in towards her as if waiting for a whisper. But there was no whisper, just Terry and her camera in the silver light. She put her camera down for a moment and turned around. When she did, he could only look at her. He recognized her expression. He remembered that expression. That night with the vodka. The first time he had truly seen the moon.

Terry snapped his picture. That was the first one she framed.

The Phone Call

I remembered Vinay's voice, late at night when the sheets rested loose around my naked legs and my eyes stayed open, tender and reddened from thoughts of my dead father.

His voice shot through my veins like a dose of heroin. He reminded me of an angel, I swore to him as I held onto his voice, the deep brown colored voice. Or maybe the earth. He did much to steady me.

◆ ◆ ◆

I met Vinay for the first time on the fourth of July, over the phone, while I was living in Chicago. My father had just died of lung cancer and I was trying to reach my friend Kim who was working at a consulting firm in New York.

A man picked up the phone.

"She's not here right now," he said. "Can I take a message?"

I paused. The man's voice startled me. I had never heard such a beautiful voice. It wasn't the accent, so much, that made it distinct, but his tone, the way the words sounded together, the rhythmic blends of highs and lows.

38

"Hello?"

"Just let her know that Meera called. There's something important I have to tell her."

◆ ◆ ◆

He called a few days later to offer his condolences.

"I hope you don't mind that I'm calling. I lost my sister a couple of years ago so I know what you must be going through. If you need anything please let me know."

"I will," I said, and called him after the funeral to talk about what happened.

"You should come to New York for a visit," he said. "Maybe you'll feel better. I'm looking out at the city now. The skyline is incredible."

I imagined him looking out the window and directing his voice upward. I wished I was there, watching his voice lingering outside his New York window and then falling off the ledge, stopping in mid-air, before landing on the ground with a small, soft cushioned sound. I'd call up to him from the ground and ask him to speak again so that I could watch the movement all over again. Except this time I would get in the way, letting his voice graze my hands.

"Maybe in a few weeks," I said.

He called me again the next day and the next and soon he was calling me everyday, sometimes two or three times a day, and I knew that when the phone would ring that it would be him, that it would be his voice and that I would feel better.

39

We talked for hours, so many hours that neither of us knew when it was time to get off the phone until the one heard the other's quiet breathing and knew that they had fallen asleep.

One night, however, I hadn't finished telling him my story, and I cried as I listened to him sleeping. I put the phone down in anguish, and lay back in bed, disappointed and hurt that he had fallen asleep.

He realized that I was gone after a few minutes and called back, but I wouldn't pick up the phone. I listened to him leaving a message instead.

"Don't be angry with me," he said into the answering machine. "I want to hear your stories but you make me so comfortable and I'm so tired from work that I fall asleep. Please talk to me. Please pick up the phone."

I listened to him from a safe distance across the room, listening to his voice, wrapping his words around me like the comforter I held in my hands. I replayed his message on the answering machine over and over, sometimes saying the words along with him, but usually just letting him speak so I'd know the words were really his. Finally I picked up the phone, and our long conversations began again.

I tried to tell my mom about some of our conversations but she didn't seem impressed. She put some more perfume on at the stoplight, then looked at me.

"I'm glad you found someone you're interested in, honey, but you should be careful. He might want your green card."

"He's been a citizen for seven years," I replied. "Anyway, he's more than just someone I'm interested in."

◆ ◆ ◆

"I love you," he said one night as we were getting off the phone.

"What?" I said. I had been lying under my comforter.

"I said I love you,"

"Please don't say that."

"Why not? It's true. We're going to be married one day, perhaps even in the old chapel behind my house. Wouldn't you like that?"

"Yes," I said, "But we need to see each other first. Maybe we won't be compatible in person. Did you ever think of that?"

"We will be," he said.

"When am I going to see you?" I asked.

"Soon," he said.

"You said that four weeks ago."

"I know, but I need to finish some things before you come."

"I don't know how much more of this I can take. We've been talking for two months now and I think it's time that we saw each other."

"I'm just not ready," he said.

"When are you going to be ready?"

"I don't know."

"Then call me when you figure it out."

◆ ◆ ◆

The next day was the first day that the phone was quiet. I watched it, next to my bed, like an orange tree waiting for the fruit to ripen and fall off.

I read, to distract myself, taking turns between reading a few words and staring at the corner of the pages that had nothing on them. I imagined him sitting there, in those empty page corners, looking at me. His brown eyes and skin contrasting dramatically with the white pages behind him. I got my fat pencil out and began to erase him, watching his eyes disappear, then his nose, then his shapely pink mouth. The eraser shavings fell over his neck and rolled into the safety of the book's binding. One eyebrow was still left.

The phone rang.

"Friday," he said wildly. "I booked a flight into Chicago this Friday."

◆ ◆ ◆

I felt nauseous as I sat at the gate and waited for his arrival. The color continued to drain from my face until the flesh tones gathered at my feet like newborn babies, which I was too tired to feed. So I closed my eyes and went to sleep, not hearing the flights announced or the children wail or Vinay approach me.

I opened my eyes.

He was on his knees before me. His soft eyes looked at me adoringly. His two tweed bags sat on either side of him like bulldogs protecting their master. He held on to their necks. Support is what he needed- I understood- I was holding on to my chair's arm for the same reason, until I let go and put my arms around him.

"How was your flight?" I asked, as I pulled back to look at him.

He looked older than I had expected. Although he was in his early thirties, I could see dark creases fanning from the edge of his eyes to the edge of his face. And his hair -- I wasn't prepared for the shock of gray, black, and white. And he wasn't as attractive as I thought he would be. I had imagined someone rugged, with long dark hair and bold, brilliant features. Instead he was thin, boyish, with plaid wool pants and a bright blue cotton tee shirt that said LA Gear on the pocket.

I felt my face fall and quickly reached for his bag. I was afraid that I had betrayed myself.

"No, no, I'll get that." He said.

"You must be tired," I said letting go.

"No, not tired, just hungry. You must be too. Let's go get a car and get something to eat."

We walked into the rental parking lot and approached the four door white sedan. He let me in, then walked around to the driver's side. He shut the door and tried to put the key into the ignition. I could see his hands shaking despite the darkness of the car. I rolled my window down.

"Where do you want to eat?" he said.

"I don't care," I said, looking out the window.

The highway air felt good against my hot cheeks. I hadn't meant to be so curt -- I was feeling anxious. I wasn't instantly attracted to him. I wasn't prepared for that. What did that mean? Would I feel it later?

"What are you thinking about?" he asked.

"Chicago traffic."

"Don't worry. We'll get there soon."

In a few minutes we approached a small Greek restaurant on Michigan Avenue. A dark-haired man offered to valet park the car. Vinay stepped out and gave him the keys. Then he took my hand and led me inside the restaurant.

He watched me take off my coat as the waiter poured our waters. His eyes lingered on my body and then moved up to my face. He looked at me and smiled. I could tell he was attracted to me. I wished I felt the same way. I watched him as he looked over his menu. His face was actually quite nice. His eyes, nose and mouth were gently balanced and his skin was dark and smooth. The streaks of gray and white, which weaved through his hair, glowed in the candlelight. The contrast in color was beautiful but also depressing. He was graying, aging. I looked back down at the menu.

The waiter came and took our order. We both ordered a Greek salad and some wine. We handed over our menus reluctantly. What were we going to look at now? Then the waiter left us the bread-basket and we relaxed a little. Cutting and buttering bread would be a great distraction.

"This is strange," I said, "Isn't it?"

He finished buttering his bread then looked up.

"Yeah," he laughed.

"Were you nervous getting off the plane?"

"No," he said.

"How did you know it was me?"

"I had a feeling."

He held my eyes for a moment. This time I looked down and buttered my bread.

The waiter came and gave us our food and we ate quickly and said little.

He took my hand again as we left the restaurant and approached the first of a series of shops on the side of the street. We stopped in front of one of the shops so I could get a better look at the jewelry box displayed in the window. The box was lit up and I could see it was made of mahogany. A sweet, smooth, dark wood. It reminded me of Vinay's voice. He saw me looking at it, and went inside to buy it for me. When he came out, he pulled me into the dark spot between the first and second shop and kissed me. I kissed him back, but I resented it. I wasn't ready. Although his voice was familiar, his body was not. He sensed my resistance and pulled me back into the street light.

"Do you want to get a drink?" he asked.

"Would you mind if we just went home instead? I'm feeling tired."

"Okay," he said quietly. And we walked back to the restaurant. He kept his hands in his pockets. When we reached the restaurant, the valet brought our car around to us. Vinay handed me the package, then started the car.

◆ ◆ ◆

We walked into the hotel room and put our bags down by the bed. Vinay opened up the small tweed bag and pulled out his toothpaste and brush. He went into the bathroom and left the door open as the water ran.

"Do you want to go to an art museum tomorrow?" I asked him as I looked for my hairbrush.

I felt comfortable with him again now that it was just our voices. Perhaps we should spend the rest of the weekend like this – me talking to him from my seat on the bed while he stayed in the bathroom. But he could only brush his teeth for so long, I thought sadly as I heard him turn off the water. Then there was no noise. I got up to check on him.

He was standing in front of the mirror combing his hair. I watched him do it, his head was tilted slightly down and the light caught the small spot on the top of his head that was hairless. I hadn't seen it at dinner. A few more strands came out as I watched. He looked up and caught my eyes.

"You think I'm ugly, don't you?" he said.

"Of course not," I said. "I just need time to get used to your body. For a long time it's just been your voice."

He walked past me and lied down on the bed. The TV was on. I lied down next to him. It was a movie: "Indecent Exposure". I had seen it before and I knew he had too because we had talked about it last week. But he stared at it as if he had never seen it before. So I went to the bathroom and put my nightgown on -- blue, his favorite color. Then I got on top of him and kissed him, lifting his hands and putting them on my breasts. His hands were dark and warm against my skin-- but they were also still.

"Fine," I said. And opened up my side of my bed. I pulled my pillow closer to my side and waited for him to say something. But he didn't. When the movie was over he reached for the light and said goodnight.

The room was black now except for the city lights. I could hear him breathing and thought about all the nights on the phone when I had heard it across the country. Now here he was next to me and we still weren't touching.

I crossed the room and went to the window and sat down in front of it, wrapping the curtain around me while I looked out at the skyline. Why didn't I feel anything? I pulled my knees closer to my chest and cried. I tried to muffle the sounds with the curtain but it didn't help. I heard Vinay move again and then get up.

He opened the curtain and kneeled down beside me. "Come to bed," he said, and took my hand and led me back. He covered me up and kissed me on the cheek, then he turned his back to me and went to sleep.

"He's given up on me," I thought and went to sleep.

The next morning we woke up and I went to the bathroom to brush my teeth. When I came out he was packing his things.

"What are you doing?" I asked.

"Packing," he said. "I'm leaving after lunch."

"Don't go. I thought we were going to go to the museum?"

"No. I need to get back," and he went back into the bathroom to take his shower.

We had lunch near the Greek restaurant from the night before. I asked him about his family and India while we ate, but he said little, choosing instead to talk about the architecture of the city. Then we headed for the airport.

"I'm sorry," I said, once we got to his gate. "I'm sorry that things didn't go the way you thought they would. But I'm not ready to give up. We just need more time together."

He looked up at me and stepped in closer. For a moment

I thought he was going to change his mind, but instead, he reached for the tweed bag that I was holding.

"I enjoyed our conversations," he said. Then boarded the plane.

There were no messages from him when I got home, or the next night, or the next. Eventually, I stopped expecting any.

After a year, I accepted a job offer at UCLA. I packed up my apartment until all that was left were three items in the bedroom: my bedding, the phone, and a small box underneath my bed. I pulled it out to look inside. There, tucked underneath a wad of newspapers, was the jewelry box that Vinay had given me. I held the smooth, deep brown colored box in my hands and remembered his voice.

Silver Boxes

The silver boxes were spaced evenly in the room like the row of silver teeth in the back of my grandfather's mouth. I had seen his silver teeth looking polished, shiny, smooth in the two black and white pictures my father had kept in his light brown lizard skin wallet. In both pictures Grandfather was laughing.

The silver boxes were much bigger here, though, in the basement of the university's science building. And the contents were different. Six dead bodies that were being examined by this year's class of medical students.

My best friend, Jeanette, had persuaded me to visit her "person," referring to the cadaver she was assigned to work on. She had been in medical school for six months, while I was working at UCLA, and this was the first time I had seen her since she started classes.

We had gone to some Halloween parties the night before. Dressed up as dead Miss America contestants who had lost the competition and were taking revenge. She asked me to go that night but I said no. She said she'd try again in the morning.

So now it was morning, Jeanette was still wearing her Miss New York sash and using the restroom. I was brushing my teeth. I put my brush down and picked up a tissue to get at the leftover blood still stuck in the corner of my eye.

"How about after breakfast?" she said, as she grabbed another tissue to cover the handle as she flushed the toilet. Her medical school courses were making her more paranoid of germs than she had ever been. Even her own germs bothered her now.

"I don't know," I said, licking the corner of my tissue and re-applying it to my eye.

"Do you know how many germs you just put in your eye?"

"Who cares. If I can't see them they don't bother me."

"Fine. But don't expect me to be spending much more time with you with that kind of attitude. I'm scared to see the things you do when I'm not around."

She went to the kitchen to get us breakfast. Powdered doughnuts and orange juice. I really didn't want to see her "person" but I felt I should since it seemed important to her.

"O.k." I said. The blood was now gone from my eye. "I'll go. Here," and I handed her the Miss New York sash. She had dropped it by the toilet.

"Throw it away," she said. "There's a trash can outside." And she went to the sink to wash her hands before opening up the clear bag of doughnuts.

The walk over to the science building was faster than I had expected. When we got inside we took the elevator instead of the stairs even though it was only two flights down. We were both still tired from last night's parties.

The elevator door opened and I saw the red doors in front of me. No labels. No numbers. Just a red door in a long white hallway. We walked into the room and Jeanette turned on the lights. It was cold inside.

I had only seen one other dead body before this, my father's, and I couldn't help but think of him as I looked at the six metal boxes. It had been a year and a half since his funeral. There was copper on them too, on the edge of the boxes and on the door's three hinges, that I hadn't noticed from a distance. It wasn't my grandfather's teeth that the boxes looked like now, but the silver and copper cigarette box that I had made Baba as a sophomore in high school.

◆ ◆ ◆

Dr. Regis had told our class that we wouldn't be working with metal much this semester since this was an Intro to Industrial Arts class. But if we had a particular project in mind, we could talk to him about it after class and he'd see what he could do.

"Yes, Meera," he said as most of the students left. Tom, Steve and I waited by his draftsman's desk.

"I want to make a cigarette box for my dad out of metal. I researched the costs of the project and it would be within the four-dollar allowance we've each been given. I've also calculated my labor costs, and with staying after school for half an hour three times a week, I could finish it in six weeks, with time left over to do an engraving."

Dr. Regis opened his blue-lined pocket notepad.

"Very impressive, Meera. Tom. Steve. I expect the same from you," and the two boys nodded.

"How about a preliminary meeting for next Wednesday at 4:00? Meet me here in front of the jigsaw. Bring your first draft."

"Sure," I said, "I'll see you then," and picked up my burgundy backpack and went upstairs to fourth hour English class.

I met Dr. Regis the following Wednesday and kept up my schedule. I finished a beautiful silver cigarette box with copper outlining and copper hinges. I put "Baba" in the center- Arabic for "father," and wrapped it in velvet. I stayed up on Wednesday to give it to him.

He came home at about 3:00 a.m. I had been up reading *Jane Eyre* and watching late night makeovers. I wondered if Jane Eyre would have been treated better if she had gotten the power make up set for $19.95 that Morgan Fairchild was demonstrating. It made her eyes look great. I was thinking of ordering it myself.

I heard the garage door open and I turned the TV off. Baba didn't like me watching those make up shows. He said we were too young for that stuff and even our mom- at forty- didn't need it. Allah had given us brown tones in our eyes and cheeks. That should be good enough for us.

I agreed in theory but chose otherwise in practice. Allah also encouraged fixing your own problems- so I felt if I was helping a bad complexion and thin lips than I was doing what he asked of me. Plus I enjoyed wearing Covergirl face powder and Bonnie Bell colored lip-gloss. So I waited till I got to school to put my make-up on and hurried after school to take it off.

Once I forgot to take off my lipstick and Baba picked us up from school. It was the sparkling kind, purple- that faded quickly after its application, which is probably why I forgot I had it on when I got in the car. He looked at my mouth but he didn't say anything- just handed me a tissue and I pretended to blow my nose as I wiped it off. I quickly told him about algebra, that I got a 97 on Friday's test, so that he would forget about the lipstick. It had been his worst subject in school.

"Great," he said, turning right without signaling. "That's my girl," he shouted and turned up the Arabic music he had been listening to. He honked to the off beats of the song and sang out loud to the other parts. Then he stopped by McDonald's a block before our house and got us both caramel sundaes to celebrate.

◆ ◆ ◆

He looked tired sitting at the counter across from me. His eyes looked more yellow than usual and he didn't laugh much even as he turned on *The Honeymooners* and watched the show for a while. Then he brought out the rice, peas and yogurt my mother had made him earlier in the day.

"Want some?" he asked, dishing it out with a wooden spoon.

"No thanks," I said. I knew he could eat it all. Baba had a big appetite even though he was a small man. We were surprised when he told us he had gotten a job as a security guard at Rubbermaid.

They probably hired him because they thought he looked like a terrorist, with his yellow eyes and dark beard and his heavy accent.

But he was mean- he admitted it. He was mean to most people except, he said, to the ones who counted: his wife; his kids; his friends and Allah. Sometimes he forgot though, or mixed up the order, yelling and hitting us with tennis rackets, books, jump rope or car tools. But that was years ago, and since he turned forty, he mostly honored his exclusions and left mom, me and Hani, my older brother and only sibling, alone.

He had to with Hani in particular, since he was no longer at home. He had moved to California to go to college. He didn't talk to Baba much when he called- he was still pretty angry about things. Baba knew it but didn't do much about it except to get on the phone and tell Hani that he'd better get good grades, or not to bother coming home, or to call him if he needed any money.

Mom and I had forgiven Baba a long time ago for his harshness. We had seen his good moods more than Hani had- perhaps since we were female, Baba tried harder to be nice to us, although sometimes he wasn't.

The past couple of months Baba and I had been getting along unusually well. It started accidentally when I fell asleep in the living room watching Richard Simmons. Usually I tried to get to bed before he came home. I didn't want him yelling at me. But I fell asleep in the soft chair and Baba woke me up.

"Come eat with me," he said.

"Ok," I said, mostly because I was still asleep.

We talked about school mostly, but then he began to tell me stories, about Jordan, and Grandfather who had been a welder in the Ottoman army, and how he got all his silver teeth. He said there was a story for each tooth and that he would tell me one for each night I stayed up for him. So I told him I would, and I did, and I learned about Grandfather through his silver teeth as well as about Baba because he had a few silver teeth of his own.

So I gave him the cigarette box during one of those late night conversations. He had gone back to the refrigerator to get more yogurt.

"What's this?" he said, as he sat back down at the counter. He pulled out the bottom of his yellow security shirt to cradle the package. He bounced it up and down in his lap, like he had done with me as a kid, like he did with mom sometimes when they were getting along.

"Come on Baba. Just open it. You're making me nervous."

"Don't be nervous," he said, his index finger pointing at me. "It's your gift so be proud of it. I expect my daughter to be proud. Head up. Shoulders back. Proud," and he thrust his thick neck into the air and pulled his narrow shoulders back.

His movement made his potbelly stick out more, pushing the velvet package to the ground. He bent down quickly to pick it up. The stool slipped out from under him and he fell. We both laughed. Then he got back up and opened the package with his teeth. He used his canines, which were sharper and more yellow than the rest of his teeth.

"Beautiful," he said. Holding it up to the light as if it were glass. "I love it. Your grandfather couldn't have welded it better himself." And he kissed me on the cheek and shook my chin roughly.

"Good night, Baba," and I went to bed.

◆ ◆ ◆

Baba had been stubborn about not going to his check-ups so by the time they found out that he had cancer, his left lung had deteriorated. His right one soon followed and he had to quit working. I moved back to Wooster after graduating from Cornell to be closer to him. He continued smoking though, and I could hear him coughing into the night and in the morning.

He used my silver cigarette box the whole time. He'd walk around the kitchen with it, bare feet, navy cotton pajamas, chest exposed, cigarette in his right hand, my silver box in the other. I felt terrible about it and I tried to go into his room twice to get it back from him. Mom had moved him into Hani's old room because his coughing kept her up. He caught me both times.

"No, Meera," he said, his eyes yellow and wild. "It was a gift. Put it down."

"No. I shouldn't have given it to you. Those cigarettes are killing you."

"Allah is killing me and I will let him, just like you and your mom will let him."

Then he lifted himself up from his pillow and reached for his radio. "Can you get me my tape from the truck? I forgot to bring it in."

So I went outside and brought it in for him.

◆ ◆ ◆

I tried to break into his room for the third time the following Saturday before dance class. But he was already dead. His yellow eyes were open and his brown skin looked bluish. The cigarette box was next to his cold fingers. I didn't move it.

The Arabic music was still playing and his right set of fingers were twisted together as if they had been snapping along. He liked to do that, snap along, to the music, his fat, flat feet hitting the wooden floor to the off beats, yelling and cursing to the first half of the song, praising Allah, me, Hani and my mom during the second.

I decided not to go to the funeral. Hani went but left for California a few days later.

"Are you sure?" Mom asked me. We were both wearing black dresses. She looked pretty in hers. She even wore a "burka," the fabric covering some Muslim women wore on their face and head. I had never seen her wear one, except in the pictures of the early years of their marriage. She had converted to Islam for my dad's sake, but after two years of marriage she stopped pretending to believe and went back to her Catholic, Eastern European ways.

"Your father would want you to be there," she said.

"Maybe. We don't know for sure. And I don't want to go. I saw him when he was dead. I've seen enough."

So they went without me and I stayed in the house and looked through his drawers, closets and boxes until I found all of his cigarettes. Then I sat down with them, in his room, with a matchbox that said *Joe's Crab Shack,* the last place we had dinner together. I lit one up and inhaled, with my thumb and index finger strangling the mouth, my thin lips sucking at the paper and the tobacco. I breathed in hard, to fill my mouth, my lungs, my conscience with smoke, until I couldn't breathe and had to cough like he had during those last few weeks.

It was the first time I had smoked.

I finished the first one. Then lit the second. And the third and fourth until soon I was no longer breathing air, just smoke and tobacco and the wrinkled paper of those damn cigarettes. I finished one pack and started on the next, knowing I was done with each cigarette by the feel of hot ashes on my fingers and on my lips.

I played his music, too, in his room while I danced on the wooden floor like he used to do. Cursing his wife, Hani, me, Allah, then praising us during the second half of the song. I cursed him, too, because I was angry. I didn't praise him. During that part of the song I just listened and lit some more of my cigarettes.

◆ ◆ ◆

"This is Kevin," Jeanette said, her gray eyes closing a little. They closed a little when she was excited, like a lizard, with gray-green sleepy eyes. She opened the metal box and let me look. His body was exposed, his head, his chest, his legs, even his penis. Most of him had been cut into. His skin had been pushed back with pins and I could see bones, muscles and veins. The formaldehyde was making me sick and Jeanette

had warned me that it would make me hungry. She was right-
because his shredded meat looked like turkey meat and it was
making me hungry. I asked her to shut the silver box.

Then she took me to the bulletin board that listed the six
bodies, their names, ages, time and cause of death. One of them
was named Hassan Jeweid. 53. Born in Jordan.

"I want to see him," I told Jeanette.

"I don't know. Are you sure you want to?"

"Which one is he? That one, isn't it?" and I pointed to the
silver box furthest away from the door.

"Yeah, that's him. I don't think much work has been done
on him yet."

So we walked over to Hassan and Jeanette opened the box.
His face was covered and his body was intact. He was also
small, but muscular, his skin taut, but discolored. I could tell,
though, that at one point he had been brown. I could see the
color around his fingernails and they were clenched too, the
way my father's were that day I found him.

"I want to see his face."

"No. Maybe later," she said and shut the box. Medical
students began to come in so we got our stuff together and
left. We showered, Jeanette did twice, and rested on her couch.
Then I packed up my car for the two-hour trip home. I went
back inside to get my purse. Then I waited on her porch.

"Do you have everything?" she asked, in her navy sweatshirt and gray pants. She had no shoes on, and there was
snow on the patio but she didn't seem to mind. She just kept
picking one foot up, then the other, and rubbing them. I was

surprised to see her touch her feet so freely, especially with bare hands. Maybe she figured the cold had killed most of the germs.

"I want to see his face before I leave."

She looked down at her feet.

"I'm cold. Let's go inside."

So we walked back in to the apartment.

"It's not him, you know. Your dad. It's someone else," she said as she opened the refrigerator to get herself a Coke. She gave me one too.

"I know. Don't you think I know? Their bodies looked nothing alike."

"Then why do you want to see his face?"

"To be sure."

"OK," she said, pouring the rest of her Coke down the sink. "If you think it will make you feel better."

So we got in Jeanette's red Toyota and drove to the science building. The parking lot was full so we parked a couple of blocks away and walked though the snow.

There was no one in the basement room, except for the six silver boxes. Jeanette went to Hassan's and unlocked it, then lifted the heavy metal door above her head. She called me over.

I approached the body and looked again at the brown by his fingernails. It seemed so familiar.

"What did he die of?"

"Lung cancer," she said and held my hand. Then she lifted the white sheet from his face. It wasn't Baba. It was someone else. They looked nothing alike. I wept anyway.

Jeanette put the sheet back on his face and was about to shut the case.

"Wait," I said, and bent over Hassan. I put his cold, clenched hands in mine and kissed it.

"Goodbye, Baba."

My kiss seemed to make his hand warmer than when I had first touched it. Perhaps it was my imagination.

Jeanette put the sheet back on his face, then shut the case. As we walked outside, it began to snow again, covering the streets and cars.

Water, Water Everywhere

I lived alone, by choice, in Harlem, in a building called International House that offered "affordable short-term leases to young adults new to New York." Mostly foreign students lived there, people who would otherwise have a hard time securing a place in the city. It was two blocks from Columbia University.

It was my first time living in New York and living alone. I had been accepted into New York Law School, which was a second-tier law school. I hadn't done well on my LSAT and was just glad to have gotten in at all. My mom felt otherwise.

"How come you didn't get into Columbia Law? You graduated from Wellesley."

"I don't know, mom," I said, chewing on some baby carrots. "It was probably my LSAT score. You know that I don't do well on standardized tests."

"You just didn't study," she said, putting the receiver down to stir the broccoli. She always made broccoli for dinner on Thursdays. Even though I wasn't there, I could see her, hand on the phone, then on her back, then on the counter, then on the broccoli, then on the phone, then on her back, then on the counter. It used to make me dizzy to watch as a kid, until I bought a Walkman and watched her do it to music.

"Of course I studied. I took that damn prep course and studied all summer. You watched me do it."

"Well, it obviously wasn't enough."

"If you think getting in is so easy, maybe you should apply."

Then she hung up on me. Typical response.

Once my mom and I went two months without talking. She had called my dad a "bitch."

"He's effeminate and whiny," she said.

I loved my dad very much and always thought my mother was being unfair to him. My dad was thin, blondish, with orange skin undertones, long neck and fingers, long legs, liked to wear argyle. Taught math.

He divorced her when I was five because she neglected him. He re-married, quickly. Some Dutch woman he found in the back of *The Enquirer*. We hardly spoke to him once he got married. Mom would get mad if we did and within eight months we couldn't - Dad refused to speak English and moved to the Netherlands.

I e-mailed him a letter shortly afterwards asking him how he was, and if he was doing pot, and to please explain why he left so abruptly. I know he read the letter because I made sure I got an e-receipt. He received it at 1:25am three Fridays ago. I still hadn't heard from him.

So I called Helen in Ohio and asked her if she had heard from dad.

"Sure," she said, turning down TLC. "He sent me a postcard. It was even written in English."

Helen made me mad; usually a child has a better relationship with one parent than with the other. Helen had both. While both of mine kept deteriorating.

The fighting with mom got worse while I was in law school. I think I was more stressed and I was learning more about my civil rights.

Lately I'd begun to get thirsty after a fight with her, particularly for water, which was unusual since I didn't like water much and usually preferred to drink coke or juice. Once I'd hear her voice rise and the comments begin, I'd open my cabinet, get a glass out and fill it up with water. Then I'd take a sip as she talked, then another, and another until it was the end of the conversation and either the water was gone or she had hung up.

At first, I thought it had to do with the construction going on outside of International House. I was sensitive to dust. But the construction soon ended and I was still thirsty.

Classes, too, were beginning to make me thirsty. There was a lot of material to learn, so much that I'd read four chapters of constitutional law with two glasses of water and think that I had had lunch. Then I'd have four chapters of torts and three glasses of water for dinner.

I hadn't yet made any friends in class to discuss it with. I was having a hard time connecting with the other students. I was either too tired to make the effort, or when I did try, I'd be disappointed. Twice I was approached by Susan, then Whitney.

Later I found out that each knew I was doing well in class and just wanted help with the assignments.

So I stopped talking to my neighbors when I'd get to class and just concentrated on the lecture and my water bottle that I'd fill, then re-fill, during the breaks between classes.

I also began to take baths more often. At first, it was once a week, on Sunday evening. I'd take a scented vanilla candle to the bathroom, fill the tub, light the candle and relax. Usually I'd play music - Tori Amos or Sarah McLachlan - keeping my legs and arms under water, sometimes my neck too and my chin so that my lips would graze the water like a lily pad in a small pond.

As the semester progressed and finals approached, I began to drink even more water. My mother would call and we would argue about my grades or about the relatives that I hadn't made time to see.

I'd go to class the next day, more tired than the last time, and instead of waiting till breaks between lectures, would get up, even as the professor spoke, pushing through chairs, papers, my obnoxious classmates, the steel door, until I got my empty cup under the clear, cold liquid pouring from the water fountain and then down my throat.

I was feeling worse and I couldn't figure out why. I knew I had chosen to be in New York, chosen to be in law school, which made me angrier with myself for feeling the way I did. "Many people would consider my life a luxury," I'd say to my-self; a nice apartment, good grades, law school, the most excit-ing city in the world... but the more I tried to convince myself how great it was, the thirstier I got and the more I drank.

My loneliness didn't affect my grades - it in fact improved them. I was studying all the time since I didn't have any friends or a boyfriend. I stopped calling home too. I thought since I couldn't shake this feeling of loneliness, then I might as well feel it as deeply and painfully as possible.

I felt increasingly guilty for feeling the way I did. Nobody had died. I had no illness. I wasn't pregnant, hadn't been mistreated. My mother was annoying, but at least I had one. And yet I had a sadness that would not leave me, no matter how much water I drank or how many baths I took.

I bought seven large gallon jugs of water and stacked them against the wall in my apartment, four on bottom, three on top. The afternoon light reflected the pale color and the bottles and together they looked like an installation that might be seen at the Museum of Modern Art. Sometimes I would take a break from studying to sit on my couch across from the display and look at them.

When I wasn't drinking water, I'd have my fingers in it, or my feet, or some other part of my body, depending on the situation. I couldn't study without both hands so I bought a foot basin to keep under my desk in the apartment. I forged a doctor's note for some of my longer classes, which said that I had to soak my right foot during class in a compound of water and a soluble pain reliever. The cause acute tendonitis developed from my undergrad years of track.

All three professors believed me, and would periodically ask me after class if the treatment was working.

"It is," I'd tell them, touching my leg. "My doctor said just another few weeks."

After class and to the subway, I kept one hand in my purse, pretending for safety reasons that I had a can of mace. Actually I had gotten several plastic tubes of water that florists put on the end of roses. I'd buy the flowers regularly, leaving the flowers outside of my door to dry, attaching the plastic tubing to my fingertips.

When I was inside the subway, I'd transfer the tubing to one of my toes on my left foot. Sometimes people stared. But no one ever asked me about it. It was New York and they were probably afraid of me.

In twenty minutes, I'd be home and in the bathtub. Baths were no longer once a week, but everyday.

After my bath came dinner, with lots of water to drink, my feet once again in a foot basin, then bed, with the floral tubing re-attached to my fingers. I slept better now since my recent purchase of a queen-size water bed.

I wasn't sure why I was so attracted to water. Why I began to rely on it so much. I had grown up in the Midwest, where there was little water to remember from my childhood, other than a small backyard pool that I never swam in.

I had gone to school in Massachusetts. There was water there, but not anywhere close by, and I did not seek it out for comfort.

But now, there was something about the versatility of the liquid, the heat of it, the coldness of it, inside or outside of my body that brought me unimaginable relief.

◆ ◆ ◆

I met Daniel a few weeks later. He was a short, sturdy man in his late thirties who stocked the water jugs at the

69

Thrifty Supermarket that I regularly went to. He had a goatee. I normally didn't like goatees but his was friendly, copper-colored and fuzzy.

He had seen me before, several times, but this time he said more than hello. He asked me if he could carry my water bottles to my car. Then he asked me out to dinner.

I agreed and we had a nice time. Soon we began to see each other regularly and after a month I told him about my obsession with water.

"Better water than vodka," he laughed, as he ordered another bottle of Evian for me. We were having drinks in SoHo. When the bartender gave it to him, he opened it, put some on his fingers, then on my lips.

The first time he spent the night at my apartment he brought me a present, a giant Evian dispenser. He had ordered it from Evian's corporate office. I put it in front of the water jug displays and took a sample.

I kissed him and he kissed me back until I realized that no part of me was being submerged in water. So I cried.

"Here," he said. And put my finger into his mouth.

So Daniel became a regular habit, like soaking my feet and drinking lots of water. It was the first serious relationship that I had been in. We saw each other about once a week, and I began to radiate, because of Daniel's love, and all the water that I kept drinking.

One Sunday we were together at my apartment. We had made love on my couch and I was feeling sleepy. My face was in his chest with my fingers in his mouth.

"What's the matter?" he said, as I got up, crying. I went to the tub, naked, and I blasted the water into the tub. He came in to see me sucking on my fingers violently with both feet in the water.

"We both fell asleep," I said, without looking at him, "And my fingers came out of your mouth."

My thin legs seemed thinner against the rising water. My red hair was wet at the ends. I dipped my hands into the water and sprinkled it on my head, as if baptizing myself.

"That's okay," he said. Putting his bare arms around me. "Wouldn't it be okay if that happened?"

"No," I said, pulling away and rubbing water on my arms where he had touched me. "I can't be without my water. Please leave me alone. I need to think."

"I can't," he said. "I love you." It was the first time he had said it. It was the first time anyone had said it.

I got into the tub and put my arms around my knees. The water was only to my ankles. It had seemed deeper from the edge of the tub.

"Why?" I said.

"I think you're smart and kind and beautiful. And your skin," he said, following the slope of my back with the edge of his hand, "You have the most beautiful skin."

My back had been to him when he said it, and I was quiet too, until the shaking I felt in my heart went into my throat and into my eyes and I turned to him, my eyes huge, my mouth open. He saw the pink flesh in the back of my throat. It was a pretty color until I screamed like a long wailing siren. He was surprised, then embarrassed for me, for himself, for getting involved with a crazy woman.

"Get out," I screamed, now standing up. "Get out. I hate you."

"Why?"

"Get out," I said, lunging towards him. "Get out. Get out."

"What did I do?"

"Get out. Get out. Get the hell out of here!!!"

And he left and I got back in the tub and let the water run. My arms around my legs, my white, sloping arms and legs getting hotter as the water rose around me, reaching for my back, my arms, my neck. I lay back in the water so that my long red hair could get wet, feeling the water from my hair fall between my shoulder blades and between my legs. I watched the warm water rise to meet my neck, my chin, my mouth and then my eyes. I closed them but I didn't have to. It was dark now and I couldn't see anyway.

Homeland Security

I.

In This One, Abdelkarim Hussein Mohamed Al-Nasser Was Clean-Shaven

She downloaded the latest photo from the *FBI's Most Wanted Terrorists* website and hung it above her computer. In this one, Abdelkarim Hussein Mohamed Al-Nasser was clean-shaven.

He had not been so in the other photos, all of which she displayed one right next to the other, one row right after another. Abdelkarim Hussein Mohamed Al-Nasser with a moustache. Abdelkarim Hussein Mohamed Al-Nasser without a moustache. Abdelkarim Hussein Mohamed Al-Nasser with a beard. Abdelkarim Hussein Mohamed Al-Nasser without a beard. Abdelkarim Hussein Mohamed Al-Nasser with a shaved head. Abdelkarim Hussein Mohamed Al-Nasser with shoulder-length hair and so on and so on.

The collage took up almost all of her wall space.

She wished the philosophy department would give her her own office so she could have four walls instead of one. She could put so many more photos on four walls. But as a departmental secretary, and with the shortage of offices on campus, she knew it would be a while.

The phone rang. The bursar's office. The reimbursement check for Professor Walsh was ready. She gathered her things and locked the door behind her, looking back at Al-Nasser, though the door was now closed.

◆ ◆ ◆

In the nineteen years that Patricia had worked at the university, she had had only two romantic prospects. One had been the Chinese bibliographic assistant for East Asian Collections. The other had been a campus telephone operator.

Angelina, the bibliographic assistant, had told her after two dates that they could no longer see each other. She wanted to marry someone from the same religion and preferably, from the opposite sex.

The campus telephone operator was a Republican.

"I'll take a cappuccino," she said to the young man behind the counter after finding out. "With a double shot of espresso."

"I'll pay for it," said a young woman to her right. In her hands were a blueberry scone and a cappuccino, wearing copper in her hair, on her arms, on her mouth.

◆ ◆ ◆

Niva's cup lay empty next to Patricia's bed. Their conversation over coffee had extended into late afternoon, then evening, then late evening and then morning. Patricia smiled as she walked over to throw away the cup. As she picked it up, she noticed three faint, copper-colored lipstick marks on the side of the cup. They overlapped each other like circus rings.

Patricia had fallen in love for the first time at the circus. While her two younger brothers laughed at the clowns and stared at the Siberian tigers, she, at thirteen, was mesmerized by the copper-covered woman riding the African elephant.

The young woman looked Salish, with long black hair and a sallow complexion and sat high on the beast, as if she owned the entire circus. The beast obeyed her. She nudged him to move forward, then stopped, nudged him to move forward, then stopped. In the bright circus lights that twinkled then dimmed, her costume glittered and dimmed as well. It was made of all copper. Parts of it hammered copper, armor-like, other parts shiny, smooth, fluid, flowing out from under the armor, down the sides of the elephant until it reached the ground.

Perhaps all the metal confused the beast or perhaps he was angry for not having all the attention. She nudged him forward but he did not move. She nudged him again and he still did not move. They stood still in the spotlight. After a few moments, he finally moved, but he jerked backwards, not forwards. The decision surprised her. She toppled over his head and onto the ground. Dust rose, then settled onto her lifeless body.

The worst part was not being able to tell her mother or the rest of the family why she had cried so hard.

◆ ◆ ◆

Patricia and Niva sat together on the warm granite rocks of the Point and opened a bottle of merlot. The grassy promontory jutted out into Lake Michigan. They sat at the edge of it and toasted the start of summer.

The sun had begun to set, glamorizing the Chicago skyline. They pointed out which buildings they knew and which ones they didn't. There was the Sears Tower. There was the Hancock.

Niva was again wearing copper. This time her dress fit tightly across her chest, then flowed out in long, gauzy pieces as she leaned against the rock. The gauzy strips rose and fell against the granite as the wind and waves came in. So did her hair. Patricia was again reminded of the Salish woman from the circus.

"For you," said Niva, handing her a bracelet. Niva worked at a currency exchange booth, but jewelry-making was what she loved to do.

"Thank you," said Patricia, putting her arm out, and admiring what she could see of the design now at dusk.

They got up from the rocks and moved back to the grass. Niva lied down and Patricia did as well, resting her head on Niva's chest with her arm still out, admiring her bracelet. They could no longer see the water, they could just hear it as the waves rose then fell against the rocks.

◆ ◆ ◆

Niva and Patricia spent most of the summer at the Point, or at festivals, movies in the park and outdoor concerts at Ravinia. By August they had decided to move in together and by September Niva had found them a place. She told Patricia before heading to a gemstone convention.

"Finally," she said to Niva. "Finally!"

"We haven't been looking for that long. Silly."

"*You* haven't," Patricia replied then kissed her goodbye as she heard the sound of the train.

Patricia walked home alone, the first time in weeks. As she passed the Japanese gardens, she reflected on their upcoming move. In just a few weeks, she was going to have a family, a home. She had not had either in many years. Two years after the circus incident, her mother had died of a heart attack while working on the assembly line. She was sent to live with a great aunt on the south side of Chicago. Her brothers were sent to an uncle in Germany. Her father had abandoned them many years ago.

She only saw her brothers once a year and her great aunt, though home for most of the day, had Alzheimer's. After she finished high school, her aunt passed away. Patricia worked at a coffee shop and struggled with what to do next, until one day her manager pulled her aside and told her that a professor had been in the other day and had mentioned an opening in the philosophy department.

◆ ◆ ◆

They had decided on a two-bedroom condo in a three-story walk-up just south of the Promontory. They had not asked anyone to help them move; with each box they packed and unpacked they quietly celebrated their happiness together.

Niva was in the bedroom now, putting a comforter on their bed and tulips in a vase. Patricia watched her from the living room. Niva looked up at her and smiled.

Patricia looked at the tulips again as Niva slept next to her, then put her arms around her and looked out the window at the skyline. There was the Sears Tower. There was the Hancock. It was as if the Point was now enclosed between their new walls. She fell asleep. A few hours later the phone rang.

"Oh, my God," said Niva.

◆ ◆ ◆

Patricia could not sleep for weeks after the news of the attacks. The terrorists, she heard, were targeting financial institutions.

She encouraged Niva to look for work elsewhere, but Niva wouldn't hear of it. She worked at a currency exchange booth, she told Patricia, not the World Bank. Plus they now had a mortgage. She wasn't about to do anything that would jeopardize their new home.

Neither would Patricia.

So the next morning she got on the Internet. What did the government advise? Then she came upon it. The FBI website. Each week it featured the most wanted terrorist for the week. It provided a photo, explained why he was wanted and described his possible whereabouts. You could even give them your e-mail address and get up-to-the-minute tips, photos and reports. She quickly typed in her information then checked her account.

They had already sent her something. This week's terrorist was Abdelkarim Hussein Mohamed Al-Nasser, originally from Saudi Arabia. Wanted for . . . they provided his profile and a photo. In this photo, he had a moustache. Patricia printed it off and put it up on her wall.

II.

Ohio Boy

Fahed Mustafa was nervous about catching his plane. It was not heights that he was afraid of, nor small spaces nor crowded seats nor even the airline food. He opened a pack of gum in the taxi and unwrapped several pieces.

By now he was Egyptian in name only. Like his parents, and even his grandparents, he had never actually been to Egypt. He thought of himself as an Ohio boy more than anything else. He hung his American flag at half staff when needed, crossed his hand over his heart at the first sound of "The Star-Spangled Banner", took the day off to vote and knew American history better than even a 10th generation American.

"Where are you headed?" asked the young man behind the airline counter.

"Cleveland. Cleveland, Ohio. I live there with my wife and daughter." He put his luggage on the scale. "Do you know which famous museum was built there in 1994?"

"Do you have identification?" the young man asked.

He handed him his passport and his Ohio driver's license.

The young man examined the IDs, then typed in his information.

Fahed could feel the line of people behind him looking at him. He was glad he had decided to wear his suit to the airport instead of his U2 sweatshirt. He rubbed his face with both hands. Damn it! He had forgotten to shave. He looked behind the young man at his reflection in the airline's mirrored logo. With his dark hair, he already had the start of a beard, making him look even more like a ….

"I didn't do it," he wanted to shout at the crowd behind him. "I had nothing to do with it! I don't know how to fly. I don't even like to fly. I have never been to Saudi Arabia. I don't speak Arabic. I don't even like Middle Eastern food. I'm allergic to most of it. Ask my wife. I'm not even Muslim. I'm an atheist!"

But he could feel the crowd staring more intensely at him the longer the young man took.

"The Irish have murdered lots of people. The British as well. The British -- the British have tried to take over the world several times. So have the Germans -- the Germans, don't get me started on the Germans," he thought as he watched a group of blonde-haired men and women walk by, reflected in the airline logo behind the counter, "and yet none of you have to be held accountable for what they did."

"I need you to step aside, Mr. Mustana."

"It's Mustafa."

"Please just step aside. Someone will be with you in a moment."

He stepped aside without turning around.

A few minutes passed.

"Mr. Mustana, please come with me."

"It's Mustafa."

"Please just come with me," the woman said as she escorted him to a back office. She asked him to sit down, then took out his ID again and punched some information into the computer. A few minutes later she looked up.

"Why are you in New York, Mr. Mustana?"

"It's Mustafa."

"Why are you in New York?"

"I'm here on business."

"What kind of business?"

"A conference"

"About what?"

"Faucet parts. I'm a manager at a plant in Ohio that makes faucets. Do you know which vegetable juice Ohio has as its state drink?"

"What country are you from, Mr. Mustana?"

"America."

"No, your real country."

"This is my real country."

"Before that."

"What do you mean, *before that*? This is it."

"Mr. Mustana, I need you to cooperate with me."

"I am. I answered your question." "I need you to please tell me which country you are from."

"I told you. America."

"Mr. Mustana, I need to know which country you are originally from."

"America. I was born in Cleveland. I was raised in Cleveland. I love Cleveland. I love America."

"I do not need to know if you love America or not. I just need to know which country you are originally from."

"I already told you."

"Mr. Mustana, I need you to please wait in this back room."

She stood up and walked around her desk. She opened the doors to her left. Inside was a small room with two chairs and a low table. On the table was a miniature American flag.

"I don't have time for this," he said, standing up. "It's Amy's birthday today. She is going to be three and I promised her that I would be home in time to celebrate."

"I understand that you may have other plans, but the country's security is at stake."

"I'm not the enemy. I didn't do anything."

"Please sit down. I need you to please cooperate with me."

"I am."

"No, Mr. Mustana, I don't think you are."

"It's Mustafa."

"That's not what the system says. The system says Mustana. It also says you are originally from Saudi Arabia."

"That's not true. I'm from Cleveland. This has already happened to me three times before. Last time it was Iraq. The time before that, Kuwait. And before that, Sudan. That's not even an Arab country. There is something wrong with your system."

"I will only ask you this one more time. Which country are you originally from?"

"America. I am American. If you took a boat tour on the *Potomac Spirit* you would see George Washington's home. New Hampshire is considered the Granite State. The Mall of America in Minnesota opened in 1992 at a cost of more than 650 million dollars. Beale Street is in Memphis, Tennessee. Interstates are only four percent of our nation's total road system but carry forty percent of all the traffic. The Washington Monument is the world's tallest obelisk. A giant sequoia tree in California is the largest living thing in the world and named for Civil War general William Sherman. *Seinfeld* is my favorite show."

They did not seem interested in his favorite show. For it was now "they" - three men had entered the room. They took him into the room with the two chairs and the low table and shut the door.

III.

The Happy List

"So this is the big time," he had said the third time they had gone out. It was July and they were at The Cheesecake Factory at the bottom of the John Hancock. Crowds of people waited inside and outside to be seated. The food passed by as they waited -- mashed potatoes and corn on the cob, BBQ ribs and chicken breasts, green beans and Asian salads in portions that could have fed three or four people.

"I've never seen such big portions," he said.

"Welcome to America," she replied.

He had been in the country for a week.

◆ ◆ ◆

"Your pros equal your cons," he told her during their first breakup. They had known each other for three weeks by then and she had pressed him as to why he wouldn't come home with her for the weekend.

"Everyone's does. It's called being human." She left his apartment.

◆ ◆ ◆

He invited her over for tea. They made love. She forgave him.

◆ ◆ ◆

Aesthetically they were well-matched — dark hair, dark eyes, fair skin – for Kyoung-mi was South Korean as well, but third generation.

She was more outgoing, however. He was reserved. She used her whole body when she spoke. He rarely raised his voice, his hands. Instead he would avoid. She preferred, even enjoyed confrontation. He did not and when he was most angry with her he would not speak to her for days, weeks.

A knock on the door.

She let him in. He looked worried.

"I feel like I'm dying," he had said. "I can't breathe." He kept checking his pulse. He had his heart monitor on.

"Do you want to go again?"

She had taken him to the hospital three times before for a similar problem. The doctors would tell them the same thing. This was a panic attack. He had an anxiety problem and would benefit from psychological treatment.

"I think you should go," she had told him. "It would help." "I don't want to date someone who suggests that I need a therapist."

She put her fork down.

"Then don't date me. But I hope you go for your own sake."

He did not go and he did not stop dating her.

He checked his pulse again.

"You're always here for me, Baby, thank you," he said, now on her bed, in her arms. She kissed him. She tried to distract him from his worries with her body.

◆ ◆ ◆

"You have an anxiety disorder," the doctor told him for the fourth time. It was always a different doctor, each time she took him to the emergency room. "You weren't having a heart attack. Though it feels a lot like it. It's a panic attack."

Quang was stretched out on the table wearing a hospital gown. She looked at him. His hair had grayed considerably in the short time she had known him. *What a shame. He's only thirty-four.*

"You're looking at my hair and thinking that I've gotten older," he said to her after the doctor had left the room.

"No I wasn't."

He had begun to take the robe off, then stopped when it was halfway down his chest and lied back down. "I used to be someone," he said looking up at the ceiling.

"You are someone."

"No, not here. Not in America."

◆ ◆ ◆

She found the happy list under his bed. It was Sunday morning and Quang had left to go back to work despite her protests. He was head of research for a finance firm downtown.

"But you're the only one who ever has to work this much. It isn't fair."

"I'm the foreigner. I have to prove myself."

"But they underpay you and you already put in seventy hours a week. No one else does."

"You just want to spend more time with me."

"That's part of it—but I also worry about your health."

He packed his bag and left anyway.

She was about to gather her things and head back to her apartment, when she found the happy list -- a questionnaire she had given him two weeks ago to help him figure out which areas in his life made him happy and which didn't. He had come to America from South Korea almost six months ago, and aside from those first few weeks she had known him, he was almost always unhappy.

"Are you happy with your partner?" the first question asked.

"No," he had written, once in English, once in Korean. She sat back down on the bed.

"How ironic," she thought, "Considering I'm the one who gave you the damn list."

She thought things had been improving, even though just two months ago they had had another breakup.

"Why?" she had asked at the time.

"It doesn't flow," he had said. "It just doesn't flow for me."

She had moved towards him for comfort, but realized, in the same motion, that he was the one causing her the pain. He kept his face in his hands. She cried by herself.

"Fine then. Go ahead and leave. I don't know why you are still here."

She continued crying and he continued to keep his face in his hands until eventually she felt his arms around her. He was crying too.

◆ ◆ ◆

She tried to pretend that she had not read the survey but she had and she was hurt and she was angry.

He was at the door now. He had come home early. She let him in. He looked at her face and he knew something was wrong.

"What is it?"

"Nothing," she replied. "Nothing."

He continued looking at her.

"I read it," she cried. "I read it! How awful! I feel so stupid! Here I am trying to help you be happy and do I get rewarded for that? No. Do I get appreciated for that? No. It has the opposite effect."

She went into the bathroom and shut the door.

"Read what?" he said. He was now on his knees talking to her through the crack beneath the door.

"Kyoung-mi-"

She did not respond.

He got up and walked around. Then she heard him picking up the papers.

"I filled this out a while ago. When I was upset with you. But things have changed since then."

"I don't believe you."

"Come out of the bathroom so I can see your pretty face."

"No," and she remained in there for another hour. Eventually, she came out and lied down on the bed next to him.

"It's not good to be, as you say, *nosey*," he said, turning towards her.

"I know. It was an accident." She began to feel better. He kissed her. He touched her. They made love.

♦ ♦ ♦

"You should make me happy but you don't," he said to her, two months later. She looked at his face. He had been tearing out pieces of his eyebrows again. His face had broken out. His face was in his hands.

"That is not my responsibility. I have already told you that. It is not my responsibility to make you happy." She got up from the bed.

He watched her walk around his apartment gathering her things. She picked up her bag when she was finished. It might as well have been a body bag, as she felt the weight of their relationship against her thighs.

"Take care of yourself," she said. "I hope you figure out what makes you happy. I hope things at work improve for you."

He began to cry.

She hugged him. They kissed. She began to cry—alternating grief and anger and frustration until till her eyes were swollen and she woke up in the morning next to him thinking this is not good. This is not good. I can tell. I can feel it. But I just can't leave him.

♦ ♦ ♦

He was cold again. He did not hold her hand. They were walking down Michigan Avenue a month later.

"What now?" she asked him.

He would not tell her.

They stopped at a café. He would still not look at her, touch her or talk to her. Finally, he spoke.

"It's not working for me. I think that I should feel a certain way about you but I don't."

"I thought we got past all this."

"I can't help the way I feel."

"But you said that last time. You keep changing your mind about me."

"I know. That's my fault. But this time I want it to stick."

She put her fork down.

"Why aren't you eating?"

"I've lost my appetite."

He took a few bites of her cookie. She would not look at him.

"If you're not going to talk then I should just take you home."

They went outside and caught a cab. She would not sit next to him nor look at him during the ride back. He kept looking at her and again as she got out of the cab and headed towards the front of her building.

"Can I call you later?"

"No," she said.

He looked upset.

"Why can't I call you later?"

"What is there to talk about? You just broke up with me for the twentieth time. Don't you remember? Does everyone in Korea have such a bad memory?"

The cab driver laughed.

Two weeks later he called her.

"I miss you," he said. "I miss talking to you."

He came over. They talked. They made love.

◆ ◆ ◆

He told her he would be leaving America at the end of the month. At the end of October. And he had not asked her to go with him.

"To Seoul or Kunsan?"

"Seoul," he answered.

She continued looking at the seam of the tent.

They had come to the park to see the Indiana Dunes—twenty-five miles of dunes along Lake Michigan, some bare and some forested. Some, they'd been told, were as low as two feet; others as high as one hundred and twenty. Since neither of them owned a car, they had taken the South Shore commuter train from Chicago, and were disappointed when the ranger told them the actual dunes were too far to walk to from the station. They had had to set up their tent and gear in the forested part of the park.

Once the rain began, they had retreated into their tent and turned on a flashlight. Then as the flashlight was dying, Quang put on a cooking light—the kind worn around the head when cooking at night. He looked funny with the light on around his head telling her such serious things. If she weren't so upset, she would have laughed. Instead, she tried to avoid his face altogether.

"My attacks have gotten worse, as you know. And our relationship. You know. The ups and downs."

"*Your* ups and downs," she thought to herself as she continued looking at the tent's inner seam.

"Are you going to date while you are away?"

"I might want to."

"Are you going to come back?"

"I don't know."

She closed her eyes.

"What are you doing? I can't see you," he said.

She felt his hand on her thigh. She could tell he was reaching out to her, not for sex, but for forgiveness. She could not give it to him. She pushed his hand away.

He pulled away and huddled too in his own corner. The cooking light was out.

A few hours later they woke up to rain. Not just the sound of it but it actually falling on their faces. The tent seam had come undone. The sky was visible. He would be gone soon, she thought, looking up at the half-open space. She looked over at him trying to fix the seam. But she could tell by looking at it that it was permanently broken.

◆ ◆ ◆

Upon advice from her friends, she tried to enjoy the last few weeks of her time with him but she was upset with him for leaving her. Her body gave her away.

She was running a fever and coughing constantly. Her body would shake after each coughing episode. He was worried about her and would lie down next to her as she coughed, keeping his arms around her to absorb some of the shock.

She looked up. His apartment was in disarray. Books, boxes everywhere. All the pieces and parts of his life, their life, in America for the past two years.

"I need to go home for a while," he whispered. "I need to figure out my work situation—how I can find happiness in my work. And my health. I need to correct my health."

She coughed again.

Partly true, she thought. She knew that he is also leaving because of her. She knew he does not really love her.

◆ ◆ ◆

He called her every day from Seoul, making arrangements to speak to her before she went to work or sometimes surprising her with a phone call at work. He told her he had purchased a ticket to come back to Chicago and would be back in three weeks. Later that night, he called her again.

"There's a problem with my visa," he said.

"What kind of problem?"

"I was on a work visa through that Chicago firm but you -- I mean your country has changed its visa laws and it's now expired."

"What does that mean?"

"I don't know. I have to talk to the embassy and find out what to do."

The next afternoon.

"They told me it is going to be hard for me to come back even on a tourist visa because I'm unemployed, but I know the real reason. I'm from South Korea and with all that just happened in New York..."

She kept listening.

"I'm going to have to find work here and stay for a while before I can even apply for a tourist visa. The only other option is a fiancé visa…"

"I don't want to agree to that unless it is from the heart."

He paused.

"I understand," he said.

And she knew he was still ambivalent about her.

◆ ◆ ◆

Their weeks apart became months and still they would not grant him a visa. She suggested she move there, but he would not hear of it unless they were married, and the same problem arose.

"We just need a few more months together to figure this out," she thought to herself as she walked back home. But her government did not seem to want to give it to them. It was now nine months since she had seen him. And yet, she was happier than she had been in the whole time she had known him.

"Where were you yesterday morning?" he asked the next time he called.

"I was interviewing for a new job."

"Why didn't you write me back?" he asked the following week.

"I joined the Sierra Club. We took a camping trip to Michigan."

"I don't know how long this is going to take," he said to her on Sunday.

She did not respond.

"Kyoung-mi?"

"It's too late," she said. "It's too late," she said again. "Or perhaps we just never had it. We were always more of an 'almost'. And 'almost' never makes anyone happy. You knew it sooner than I did. You knew it three weeks into this. When you first broke up with me. When you love someone, when it is genuine, you see their flaws but they are not flaws -- they are endearing. To you they were always just my flaws. My pros equaled my cons. You could write them all out on paper. You could have made an excel sheet out of them. In fact, you probably did."

"No. It was not your responsibility to make me happy."

"But it is my responsibility to make myself happy. I moved to this city with dreams and hopes of my own and those were all put aside when I--"

"Met me?"

"Yes. But that was my--"

"Responsibility."

"No, choice. It's always about choices -- and faith -- faith in the unknown. Having faith that it will work out without knowing what is next gives you the strength to make the choice."

"And you are choosing to leave me?"

"I am choosing to make myself happy."

"And America is helping you."

"Yes, I suppose she is. Yes, I suppose she did."

The Spanish Dancer

It might have been a party from the sound of the conversation. Ken from cardiology is describing the full frontal nudity scene in "Fight Club." Paula from pharmacy is punching Ken in the arm. Steve from nursing is telling Patty about an amazing Indian restaurant that had just opened downtown. Eleanor from neurology is recounting an unsuccessful first date. And Rosalinda, a third year resident, stands in the back and watches them all.

Like the other physicians, nurses, nursing personnel, technologists, and aids, Rosalinda is waiting here in the emergency room of Grand Rapids County hospital for the near-fatal drowning victim to arrive. They had been paged a few minutes ago and had rushed down from their respective units to help.

While the others continue to talk, Rosalinda thinks about the old Turkish woman who had been in her care yesterday. Despite being blind, she had continued to look at Rosalinda as if she could see. Perhaps, Rosalinda thought, she was one of those people who could read the color of a person's aura. She had told Rosalinda that she used to be able to read fortunes in leftover Turkish coffee grounds. The thick, black residue in the ceramic cups painted heartbreaks and babies, freezing fogs and lentil crops.

Rosalinda had wanted to paint the old woman, paint those soul-seeing, color-soaked eyes. She would have done them in violet and chocolate brown. She almost said so to the attending physician, but held back. The few times she had shared her thoughts with her colleagues, they had changed the subject, or just stared at her before turning around. And painting, painting was something she had done a long time ago.

◆ ◆ ◆

Pale pink lights beam down on the limp, wet little girl as physicians and nurses lift her from the stretcher onto the emergency room table, stabilizing her neck and back. The crowd quiets as the attending physician summarizes:

"Nine year old female submerged for over twenty minutes in Ladybug Lake of Land Between the Lakes. Father pulled her out and attempted basic life support. Paramedics continued CPR in the ambulance. Oral tracheal intubation was performed as well as external cardiac massage. Victim is currently unresponsive and appears to be comatose."

The child's vital signs are taken, blood samples drawn, IV fluids administered. A few minutes go by, but the girl remains blue. All Rosalinda can do is stare -- the girl looks exactly like she had at that age.

"Cardiac arrest. I.V. Push 2cc's 1:10,000 stat!"

She even has on the very same Superman swimsuit
Rosalinda had worn as a little girl -- despite her mother's
protest that Superman was for boys. Because they did not sell
Superman swimsuits for girls, she had had to make her own.
"Diffribulate."
Paddles are applied to the girl's chest.
"Shock her – CLEAR!"
Had the girl done the same?
"Time of death," announces the attending physician, "1:27 p.m."
The girl's body is wheeled away. The physicians and nurses
returns to their departments. Rosalinda stands alone. The swim-
suit lays on the floor.

◆ ◆ ◆

After her shift, Rosalinda drives out to Land Between the
Lakes. The sun had set hours ago and she walks through the
forested promontory of oak, maple, and aspen in moonlight.
After a mile she gets to the first lake, Ladybug Lake, and
sits down on a piece of limestone. On the other side of the
promontory is Crooked Lake. In the distance she can hear elk,
moose, and white-tailed deer feeding. An owl hoots. Brown
bats swoop and dart. Three lightning bugs congregate in front
of her.

At the end of fourth grade, her class had taken a field trip
to the University of Michigan's Museum of Art. It had been
her first trip to an art museum and she had not wanted to go.
In front of them, on the main wall, was *Paris Street; Rainy
Day* by Gustave Caillebotte. On the right, pastel-colored river

100

banks, 17th century gardens and half-open irises. On the left, women napping, women stitching, women doing laundry. Then the men -- men reading, men lunching, men with their faces in their hands. She put her own face in her hands. She did not care for Renoir, Manet, or Monet, despite how enthusiastically her teacher talked about them. When her teacher began to discuss the next painting, Rosalinda left the room to find a drinking fountain. She wandered through the galleries looking for one, then paused at a painting on a blue wall.

It was a tall painting, about three feet by seven feet, of a glorious Spanish dancer. Around her flared heaps and heaps of embroidered white fabric. Behind her right ear was a flower; at her feet, some of its petals. Natalia Gocharova, a Russian-born French citizen, was the painter. The exhibition card said that she had used the Spanish dancer as a frequent theme for her paintings. Sergei Diaghilev, the famous Russian dance impressario with whom she often worked, had even conceived a production on the same theme. Gocharova designed many costumes and sets for this never-realized ballet.

"How sad," she thought. "It could have been such a beautiful ballet."

She sat down in front of the painting and continued looking at it, struck not by its texture, technique, or composition, but a feeling. A feeling of possibility.

After school, she began to paint. She didn't have many colors to work with -- just white paint leftover from her mother's living room and copper paint that her father had used on their furnace. Despite her limited palette, when the paint was put on the cardboard, the colors changed. They changed from white and copper to bright blues, greens, yellows, reds, oranges, and purples. With more colors to pick from, there, in that small attic, she began to paint some of what she had seen, some of what she had experienced. After three hours, she climbed down to join her family for dinner. She left the paintings to dry.

"Your father," her mother said to her in Spanish with two of her three brothers attempting to climb into her lap, "will be late tonight."

Relieved, she took a sip of tamarindo water.

◆ ◆ ◆

"Get up!" Her father shouts the following morning. "We're going swimming!" They all wake up and look at him, then laugh. He already has his goggles on. Rosalinda hurries to get ready. It is rare for them to be going on an outing. It is rare for her father to be in a good mood.

It is her first time at The Land Between the Lakes and Ladybug Lake feels good as she gets in. She takes her time with her strokes, practicing what she learned at the Y's after school program. As she begins the breast stroke, she looks up at the sky. Peach clouds float by and she thinks about how she can replicate them on canvas. Maybe her father would let her have some of his paint. Then she looks away from the sky to the edge of Ladybug Lake. Her young mother is trying to assemble their picnic, batting at her three small brothers as if they were mosquitoes. She laughs, then thinks about putting that scene on canvas.

A few minutes later, she gets out of the water and approaches the blanket. Her mother hands her a plate of chicken salad, grapes, and two buttered rolls.

"No, thank you," she says. "I want to paint first."

"Paint what?" demands her father. He looks different now. Different than he had in the car.

"The clouds and maybe all of you, like this, eating."

Her father puts his plate down, his olive face darkening, both arms shaking.

"There's already one painter in this family."

"I want to be a different kind of painter. I want to paint what I imagine, not just other people's houses."

Her father pushes her mother over and crawls over to her, putting his right knee in her chicken salad.

"I do not slave away on white people's house for twelve hours a day for you to become a painter," he says to her in Spanish then hits her backhanded across the face. If you are to become anything, it will be a doctor. Now eat your chicken. You are not allowed back in the lake until you eat your chicken."

She looks to her mother for help, but her mother just smiles. No matter what her father ever says or does to them, her mother just smiles.

Rosalinda turns her back on her family and holds her face.

When she gets back in the water, she does not look up at the clouds or at her family's picnic. She looks down into the water, her spirit slipping to the bottom. Back home, she climbs up into the attic and looks at her paintings. They are merely two colors on cardboard.

◆ ◆ ◆

Rosalinda's next shift at the hospital will begin in a few hours. She sits on the limestone a while longer. The fireflies are fading. Now the sun is rising. A white-tailed deer feeds behind her.

She stands up and begins to gather her things. As she searches for her hospital badge, she notices movement in Ladybug Lake. She looks out at the water. Nothing. She walks to the edge of the water. Stillness. She walks in anyway. Still nothing. She walks in further, the water now up to her waist. Again, nothing. She waits. She sees it again. Again it disappears. She decides to retreat when something touches her ankle. She reaches down and grabs it. It is still moving even as she pulls it out of the lake. Algae. A huge clump of algae. For a moment she had thought it would be something else. For a moment, she thought it would be the girl's swimsuit. Her swimsuit. Their swimsuit. The algae is limp in her hands and she thinks, "haven't we been underwater long enough?"

She climbs out of the water and gets back on land. She takes two breaths and turns around.

The scene behind her has changed. It is still morning but Ladybug Lake is gone. She turns to the other direction. Crooked Lake is also gone. Where there had been two bodies of water there is now just land, and trees -- maple, poplar, aspen-- and look, a dogwood tree. The dogwood, the largest of the trees, was full of heaps and heaps of white flowers. It reminded her of something. Yes, the Spanish dancer. She was again looking at the Spanish dancer with petals at her feet and white fabric all around her. She would paint her once she got home. She would paint again when she got home.

Nuclear Energy

Harriet Motley had started off in the café when the building had first opened and had done very well, learning the menu not only by heart, but also in French. The International House program director had been at the café one afternoon and overheard her. A Parisian himself, he was amazed at her near-perfect accent.

"How did you learn to speak French like that?" he asked her.

"My mother was from Ghana," she replied before unbuttoning her red wool coat. "I can also speak Italian and Japanese. Those I taught myself."

Now, at twenty-six, she was the first black woman to hold a desk job at the International House of Chicago. Her responsibilities, the program director told her, were to answer the phone and to greet the guests, check them in, and answer whatever questions they may have about the building.

Built ten years ago by John D. Rockefeller, Jr., the Gothic-style building was located on the University of Chicago campus near the Midway Plaisance. Faced with Indiana limestone, the structure had nine stories and a tower rising twelve stories. Inside was a courtyard, men's and women's social rooms, a main lounge, a reception room, an assembly hall, the main dining room, the café, and the dormitories—half of them for men, half of them for women.

The dormitory rooms themselves were small, about eight feet by six feet with one window, a desk, a twin bed, and a few shelves for books and things. Despite the size of the rooms, there was almost never any vacancy at "I-House" (as it was nicknamed). The construction of the building had gotten a lot of publicity and the concept was enticing to American and foreign visitors alike—a chance to live with students and scholars from around the world.

Now it was March of 1942 and neither the visitors nor the staff of International House were interested in anything besides the war in Europe. Dale, Harriet's fifty-year old supervisor, had pulled her aside yesterday and told her that a group of scientists would be staying at I-House. They were coming to campus to work on a project and would be arriving tomorrow.

"What's the project about?" asked Harriet.

"It's a secret. Even I don't know the details," said Dale. "And I may not be around when they decide to tell me." She knew then that he really had no idea. Whenever he was excluded from something important he threatened retirement.

◆ ◆ ◆

"I'm here to check in," said a small, blonde man in his early thirties. His hair was cut close to his neck and ears and he wore his white shirt open at the neck, revealing smooth, hairless white skin. His pants too were white and he would have looked like a Norwegian bride if not for his eyes. His eyes were black, very black, the same color as the onyx ring he wore on his right hand.

"Gavor Zsolnay from Hungary."

Harriet took his paperwork and began to process it.

"I'm going to be working at the Met Lab."

"Excuse me?" she said while typing.

"The Metallurgic Laboratory. Part of the Manhattan Project. We're trying to build an atomic bomb."

She stopped typing.

"Is there a problem?" asked Dale, coming out from the back office.

"No, Sir," said Gavor. "But I do think you should give this intelligent woman a raise."

She laughed and finished processing his paperwork.

◆ ◆ ◆

The following evening Gavor stopped by Harriet's desk before going up to his room.

"Remember what I tell you yesterday?"

"Have we met?" she asked.

"Good girl," he said laughing before continuing. "It really is a secret. It's just that I have a wide mouth and am so proud of the work we do. Will you promise me you won't say anything to no one?"

"Does that include the *Tribune*?"

"Very funny," he said, laughing again. "Smart girl." And he wished her good night.

◆ ◆ ◆

He began to stop by her desk on a regular basis. Her shift ended at ten, and because he often stayed late at the lab, she had usually gone home for the night. But when he did manage to catch her at her desk, he would tell her about the project while she filed the last of her paperwork or put away some keys.

"We're getting close," he said a few weeks after moving in, diagramming the atom for her on the back of his hand. "But we have to find a way to slow down the neutrons."

Two weeks after that, he said, "we can't figure out the minimum amount of uranium needed to sustain the reaction."

Then there would be weeks where he would say nothing at all, just walk tiredly by her desk and wave goodnight.

◆ ◆ ◆

"I bring delicious food," he said to her a month later. In his arms were several dishes and a bottle of white wine.

"What's this?" asked Harriet.

"Hungarian appetizers. This one is *sult libamaj*, or goose liver slices; this one *hortobágyi palacsinta*, or hortobágy pancakes; that one *körözött juhtúró*, or spicy ewe cheese; and this one, my favorite, *töpörtyûs pogácsa*, or pork crackling scones."

"What are we celebrating?" she asked, sampling a pork crackling scone.

"Today we isolated the first pure sample of plutonium," he said while opening the wine.

"Congratulations," she said and toasted to his success.

"The recipes for these dishes come from Kalocsa, my hometown in Hungary. The main ingredient is paprika—which as you may know, has made Hungary famous."

"I know about paprika. My mother often used it in her cooking."

"Well, give her my recipes! Maybe she want start using it again."

"I can't," she replied. "She passed away a few years ago."

"I'm sorry--" Gavor began.

"Let me try a goose liver slice," she said quickly.

"That's one of the simplest recipes," Gavor responded extra cheerfully, noticing her expression. "Just get fresh goose liver, fry it in some fat, water and onions, then, when it is almost done, sprinkle it with paprika and parsley."

"Very good," she said, reaching for another one and hoping to redirect his gaze.

"One of the most beautiful views in Hungary is also from my hometown," he continued. "It is the sight of long strings of paprika hung on the white walls of the small houses along the Danube River."

He took out a photo and showed her. Then he showed her another one and another one until their appetizers were gone, the wine was gone, and it was time for Harriet to go home.

◆ ◆ ◆

Harriet began to check out books about nuclear physics from the university's library. She read the first set of books she borrowed over the weekend then returned to the library to get more. This time she checked out books on chemistry.

Gavor continued to confide in her about the details of the project. Eventually, she was able to not only comprehend almost everything he told her, but could offer him feedback as well.

"The biggest problem we have right now," he said, "is finding a suitable neutron moderator." He listed the ones they had already tried. Harriet looked at the list written in pencil.

"What about graphite?"

He looked at his pencil.

"You're right. You're absolutely right. That's it! That's it!" He kissed her on the cheek and ran back to the lab.

◆ ◆ ◆

"Would you like to see it?" he asked her a few weeks later. It was now early December.

"I would love to," she said.

"I wait in the café till you are done with your shift."

◆ ◆ ◆

The experiment was being conducted in a doubles' squash court beneath the stands of Stagg Field, the University's abandoned football stadium. Inside the squash court, a giant, square balloon had been unfolded and hung from the ceiling with one side left open. In the center of the rubberized canvas, layers of graphite blocks were being alternated with layers of graphite blocks with uranium bored in. The entire structure was spherical, with a diameter of about twenty-four feet.

Harriet watched as the scientists passed blocks from one to the other, being particularly careful with the blocks containing the uranium, until another layer was complete. A certain amount of uranium was needed to sustain a chain reaction. Less than the amount needed (and not much was needed at all) and an explosion could occur. The perfect formula they were hoping for was known as critical mass—and the scientists knew they were very close to reaching it.

"Maybe just another layer or two," said Herb Anderson, one of the young scientists piling graphite up near the top of the ceiling. He looked again at the instrument's counter.

"Then what?" asked Harriet.

"Well, there won't be a 'then what' tonight," Herb replied. "Enrico told us to continue layering till the fifty-first layer, put in the rods, then go home. We're not allowed to start the experiment without him."

"What layer are you at?" asked Gavor.

"Fifty and the instruments are going crazy. See that control rod over there?"

Gavor nodded.

"After one more layer, all you would have to do to get the reaction going is pull that rod out, one, maybe two feet."

"Enrico would kill you."

"It's tempting, isn't it?"

It was almost midnight now and most of the scientists had already gone home. Herb finished layering the fifty-first layer, made some calculations, put in the safety rods, and then walked over to Gavor.

"I'm heading out. Just lock up when you get done." He handed him his clipboard, then said goodnight.

112

Most of the lights in the court had been turned off after the scientists left and it was now just Gavor, Harriet, and the world's first nuclear reactor. Gavor excused himself to make a phone call. She was now alone with the reactor.

Her mother had worked hard to educate her. Alone and in a new country, most of that education had taken place among dry cleaned coats during her mother's shifts.

"I am my mistakes, Harriet, just as much as my successes," her mother had said to her one day. She had been sitting under her mother's red, wool coat, a coat that had been her mother's before that.

Harriet thought about the funeral as she looked at the pile before her now. The pile of graphite and uranium reminded her of the pile of dirt on her mother's grave. She had been told it would settle a few weeks later, but it never did. Even when she went to visit a year later, the earth was still piled high above her body-- a constant reminder that some types of pain never do settle.

She took off her coat and began to climb the pile. Climbing to the first then fifth then tenth layer till she got to the fifty-first layer, and began to dismantle it, taking the first block of graphite from its position and pushing it over the edge. Then the next and the next until she was halfway through the fifty-first layer. She had just begun to work on the second half of the layer when she saw Gavor, running towards her.

"Put it down. Put it down. You're going to ruin the experiment!"

She kept going. Throwing the graphite blocks and pieces of uranium over the edge as quickly as possible. More men entered the room. She kept going, throwing the graphite and uranium pieces over the edge till they came down like black rain-- no, that would come later. The men grabbed her. She lost her balance. The men pulled her down. The lights came back on.

* Nuclear Energy named after Thomas Moore's monument by the same name at the University of Chicago. It was built to commemorate the world's first controlled chain reaction.

The Invention of Television

He had been raised in the same house that television was invented in, though he found out later that no one had actually invented television. It was more of a collective effort. Nevertheless, Charles Francis Jenkins had lived here, in this house, in this town outside Richmond, Indiana. In 1923 he transmitted moving silhouette images and in 1925 publicly demonstrated synchronized transmission of pictures and sound. On June 30, 1925, he was granted U.S. patent No. 1,544,156 (*Transmitting Pictures Over Wireless*).

Despite her pride in the house's historical significance, his own mother - not Jenkin's mother, for it was now 1978 - did not actually let him watch any TV. She did not let him do much at all nor did she spend much time with him at all. Most of his time he spent either at school or at home alone watching shadows on the wall. The only thing that consoled him, while he sat there at the foot of his bed, was the thought that perhaps this is what Jenkins used to do as well.

His mother, on the other hand, spent most of her time in the kitchen. Not actually cooking anything -- rolling dough or pinching anything -- just in the kitchen with her head in the oven.

"Is that on?" he screamed the first time he had come home and seen her doing it.

"No," she said, without removing her head to talk to him. She provided no further explanation.

So he grabbed some chips and a coke from the fridge and went back to his room.

Shadows again, he said to himself. And cleared a space on his bed, then a space on the wall for the afternoon light to come in. He again watched shadows moving on the wall.

If only they could talk, he thought to himself. Which is perhaps what Jenkins had thought. Which is perhaps what had given Jenkins the idea.

The sun was beginning to set. The shadows disappeared as they merged with the darkness. Charles leaned back against the foot of his bed and thought about his mother. Perhaps the oven had come like that. With his mother's legs sticking out from the bottom and her back bent over like a wooly ski slope and her dark hair parted down the middle. Or maybe it was the other way around, his mother had come like that, with the oven firmly attached to her head and he had been too young to notice.

It was unusual for him to come home and not see her as a part of the oven, though one afternoon he had.

"Hello, Mother," he had said, combing his hair straight before walking through the door. She disliked curls—both his and hers.

"Hello, Charles," she said looking at him from the living room till she registered that he had come home. Though she did not care for the fact that Charles Francis Jenkins had contributed to the invention of television in this house, she liked the name and had named him Charles after the semi-famous-but-still-obscure individual.

Then she again bent into the oven.

The least she could have done was to have had another child so I would have someone to talk to, he thought to himself. But that would involve a man. And his mother seemed allergic to anything male - no male pets were allowed, no male visitors, no male plants, even.

"But how do you know they're male?" he had asked her once. She was getting ready to return two plants to the store.

She took a moment to re-part her hair then spoke.

"Male plants usually flower first. The flowers come out on a fairly thin stem that extends up above or out below from the branch or vine. See?" She took some of the pollen from the stamen and showed him. "We know this one is ready because the pollen came off on my finger."

"And the female?"

"The female flower will be close to the vine and the stem will be a lot shorter than the male stem. In the center is the 'stigma,' which must receive the pollen in order for the fruit to develop. See how this flower is open? It is a mature female ready to accept pollen."

He had wanted to ask her some more questions but the lecture was over. Her eyes were now half-closed. Her hair, disheveled. Instead of returning the plants to the store, she put them in the sink and opened the oven door.

His homework was finished. He was tired of his three games. He had no TV. If only I had a TV, he thought, it would all be so much better. But he was only eleven, with no financial resources other than a nickel that he now turned and twisted in the air to create currency shadows on the walls.

"If only I had a nickel that big. I bet the Federal Reserve would want to buy it from me and then I could purchase a television." He lay back down for a minute. Then he smelled it.

Cabbage. Cabbage again.

His mother made cabbage almost every night. He didn't understand why. She wasn't German or Polish, Romanian or even vegetarian. "Part Cherokee," is all she had told him.

"Time to eat!" she hollered.

He went into the kitchen and sat down at the table. His mother had gone to her bedroom and had left him pork loins, cabbage and a glass of water. He ate quickly then went back to his room. Again, he cleared a spot on his bed. Again, he cleared a spot on the wall.

He got up to open the curtain -- but alas. He had forgotten. It was now night. No light. There would be no shadows on the wall.

"I'll create them. I bet Charles had to do that as well."

He took down his lamp. He got a sheet from the closet. He laid the sheet over the lamp. The light went out. Darkness.

"What happened?"

They had lost electricity. It now began to rain.

"I can't take this anymore! I can't take this anymore! I can't take this anymore!" He began screaming.

His mother came into his room. The first time in as long as he could remember. She stood in darkness, remaining in darkness while figuring out what to do. Then lit the candle she had in her hand. He was lying in bed. She came and sat down next to him. She placed the candle in a glass on the table to her right. She cleared her throat, and began to sing to him while keeping one hand on his chest.

The next day, when he came home, there was a television in his room. A big one, too. Almost twenty-five inches across. He had taken out a ruler and measured it.

"Thank you!" he said, running back to the kitchen. "Thank you!" But his mother had already put her head back into the oven.

He went back to his room and turned on the TV. It was Friday -- only Friday. He would have the whole weekend to enjoy it. Great! He moved the TV right in front of his bed and got under the covers, watching one show after another for the rest of the evening and into the night. By morning the sun was out, shadows were again on the walls but he ignored them. His mother called out that breakfast was ready. He ignored her too. A game show had come on. He turned up the volume then slammed his door.

The Ice Storm

She awakened to a popping sound and for a moment thought her dead husband was back in the room with her. But it was not Joseph. It was the ice breaking outside.

Her dark room lit up blue and then orange as the electrical transformers on the streetlights shorted. She went to the window to watch but the streetlights were already down. By moonlight she could see them, jutting out from the ground broken and smoking. Even the sky was covered in ice. She put her face against the glass. No, not the sky. That was ice on the window still accumulating as rain hit and froze on contact.

She lit a candle and headed to the utility room, passing Joseph's paintings from Iran. She stopped and looked at the pomegranates, half-open figs, lemons, and oranges hung up and down the hallway. Even in candlelight their colors were vivid— dark reds, yellows, greens and oranges. She put her face close to the paintings but it was paint, not fruit, that she smelled.

On the other side of the hallway were prints she had brought back from Hungary -- much different in style. Not only because they were Hungarian, and prints, but also because they were of the late Gothic period. She stopped and looked at "Churning Woman," by Mihály Munkácsy. The old, tired woman had reminded Anne of her Hungarian grandmother. Later, as her mother had aged, it had reminded her of her. And now, as she passed the hallway mirror, it reminded her of herself.

"Joseph would not like me looking like this," she said again out loud. But she did not mean it, for Joseph had admired her his whole life.

Within a few minutes she had entered the garage and was kneeling in front of Joseph's cabinet.

"No," she said. "No," she said again out loud. It was hard for her to be so close to his things. One drawer after another was filled with his dentistry tools, patients' thank you letters and even their teeth. Finally, she located the radio and the flashlight. As she was getting up, she noticed something else.

The envelope, she said, this time to herself.

A large envelope with Hungarian stamps in the back of a drawer. She had not seen it in years.

She held the envelope in her hands. More popping sounds came from outside.

◆ ◆ ◆

The Gellért Hotel and Baths at the foot of Gellért Hill were famous not just in Hungary, but throughout Europe. Built in the modernist Secession style at the beginning of the 20th century, the opulent, yellow-colored building was separated into two baths—one for women, one for men. Having been in Hungary for only a week on a summer architecture program, she did not know this yet and walked into the baths on the men's side.

Inside the large, marbled area were plunging baths in a variety of shapes and sizes. Naked men, ranging in age from eighteen to seventy, were enjoying them. She did not know whether to look at them or the mosaics of burgundy, yellow, light blue and black that lined the baths, the walls, even the columns. She looked at the mosaics.

"The women's baths are over there," shouted a short, handsome man smoking between two of the columns. He was in his thirties and spoke English to her with a Persian accent.

"Thanks," she returned in Hungarian.

"You are American," he said laughing. "Why aren't you speaking English? Aren't Americans honest?"

"Yes, Americans are honest. But they also have to be careful."

"I won't hurt you," he laughed again while he wrapped a towel around himself. "I'm just as interested in staying here as you are."

He walked over.

"My name is Joseph."

"My name is Anne."

◆ ◆ ◆

It was going to be difficult to get Joseph a fiancé visa. Not only was Joseph living in a Communist country, he was originally from Iran.

"Don't blame me," she told him, tapping the calling card against the student center's public phone. "I don't work for the government."

"Maybe you should,'" he returned, speaking to her from his apartment in Budapest. "Maybe that would speed things along."

She was quiet.

"I'm sorry, Anne. I just miss you."

"I spoke with my advisor and I might be able to visit you next month."

"Next month. Next month. That is what you said last time. It's already been eight months."

"It's not my fault that they've become stricter with the visas. I do have to graduate."

"Do you love me more than you love architecture?"

"That's a silly question."

"I miss you."

"I miss you too."

"I miss your body."

She paused.

"Yes," she said. "I miss yours too."

"No, not in the same way. It is much harder for me."

"Why is that?"

"Because I'm a man."

"So?"

"Men have needs."

"And women don't?"

Two of her friends walked by but she did not say hello; she only tapped her card harder on the glass.

"What are you trying to say?"

"A man can only go so long."

"Before what?"

"You know what I mean."

"No, I don't," she said. "I have to go. I have to study."

◆ ◆ ◆

She thought about a couple she had known as a child as she walked back home. The wife had been a professor of Chinese art. The husband, a physician. The wife would have to go to China periodically for six, seven months at a time.

One night, when the wife had been at their house having dinner with her mother, Anne heard her use the word—"serviced." She told her mother that every time, before she left for her long trip, she would arrange to have her husband serviced while she was away.

It was not until Anne was older that she understood what she had meant.

She went into the kitchen to make tea, then went to gather mint from the side of the house.

She was not in China, but she was far away and he was far away and she had such little control in this situation. She couldn't make them give her a visa. She couldn't make herself magically appear.

She put the mint in her tea and watched the leaves darken.

◆ ◆ ◆

It was difficult for them to coordinate calling. Joseph was no longer in dental school but was out practicing, and she was in her final year of architecture school.

"I miss you," he said again. She worried now when he said that.

"How are your patients, Joseph? Are they being nice to you?"

"Of course, darling, but I miss you."

"I know, Joseph, I miss you too."

"Not as much as I do."

Her grip tightened on the receiver.

"I've been thinking," he said.

"Yes."

"I've been thinking…." he said again.

"Just tell me."

"I want to see someone."

"Who?"

He paused.

"You know what I mean, Anne."

"No. I don't."

"A prostitute."

She was hunched over now in the booth holding the phone against her chest.

"I'm sorry, Anne."

"I have to go," she said and hung up the phone.

Immediately, she redialed.

"Fine, Joseph. Fine. But I want to be the one to pick her out."

◆ ◆ ◆

She arranged to have photos sent to her of some of the prostitutes in the Castle District. She had noticed their building while visiting Mátyás Church. Though they had tried to build its structure similar to the buildings surrounding it, she could tell from the façade, the balcony and the molding that it was

127

built much more recently and with a different purpose.

She took the envelope into her bedroom and closed the door. It was fall now in Colorado and much colder in the house. She put on a sweater, then sat back down on the bed.

The first photo was wrinkled. She straightened it against her knee. The woman was about twenty with dark brown hair pulled back in a ponytail. Her eyes reminded her of her sister.

"No," she said.

The next woman was older. Twenty-seven or twenty-eight with short, blonde hair and blue eyes. She looked friendly. Like a nursery school teacher.

The next photo was torn. The young woman was topless. She was reclining on a couch. She held the picture closer. There were bruises around her ankles.

She put the photo down and took a sip from her drink-- not tea this time but something stronger.

The next photo—fifteen maybe. Blonde hair with dark roots. She looked like she had been crying.

She took two more sips. Quickly, she scanned through the rest of the photos. One fell to the floor, face down. She picked that one up and turned it around. The girl was about twenty five with dark hair and green eyes, wearing a red sweater. She looked a lot like—herself. She put the photo in the envelope and sealed it. Then went outside to vomit.

◆ ◆ ◆

Joseph had not commented on the girl when he had received her photo. He just said that her envelope had arrived.

Later, she had pressed him as to when he was going to meet her. He had not wanted to tell her. Last night she had pressed him some more and he told her. It would be this weekend.

It was now Friday morning and Anne had decided not to go to class. She went to the living room and began a sketch—but began sketching bodies not buildings.

She switched to physics instead, but relived the same scene. Joseph and another woman being intimate.

She closed her book and went to the kitchen to make some tea. She went out back to get some more mint. There must have been a cold front, for the mint was frosted. She got back into bed and stayed like that for the rest of the day. Night fell and the sounds changed outside. An ice storm had begun. She stayed up all night watching the ice accumulate on the peach tree outside her bedroom window. By morning, every branch, every leaf was encased in ice.

◆ ◆ ◆

They married a year later and moved to northern California. Anne worked from home while Joseph worked for a clinic in the area. Within a couple of years they had saved enough for a house in the country.

Their two-story house was on three acres—including an acre of soybeans, a small pond, a barn, a birdbath, and ten apple trees that grew in front of a low hill.

The following spring, as soon as he could work the soil, Joseph planted cherry and peach trees between the apple trees. Anne watched him from the house, digging the holes for the trees and gently placing the balled-and-burlapped trees into each one. In front of their bedroom window, he planted a date tree.

Spring ended and summer began. The young trees grew and the apple trees bore fruit. She held hands with Joseph while he picked some.

With fall came their first frost.

"I hope our trees will be okay," Joseph said, waking up and looking out the window. Frost on the date tree in front of their window reminded her of something. Yes, the girl, she remembered, and turned over.

"It's nice to be inside, though," he said, getting back into bed and holding her. He stroked her breasts. She did not respond.

◆ ◆ ◆

When spring returned, Joseph planted more trees. He added apricot, plum, and pomegranate.

Joseph and Anne sat with them under the trees, eating paludeh, a sorbet made of rice flour, grated fruit and rose water from Shiraz. Sometimes they had guests.

"This looks like Iran," Joseph commented.

"We didn't even have to get a visa," his guests joked. Above them hung cherries, peaches, and apricots.

"It's beautiful, Joseph. Just beautiful. You were born with a green thumb even though they won't give you a green card." They laughed some more.

Joseph offered his guests pistachios, grapes, watermelon. Anne reached for a grape. Joseph kissed her hand.

◆ ◆ ◆

Summer ended and fall began. Anne stared at the broken, frozen branches of the tree in front of their window. She asked Joseph to sleep in the other room.

The following night, she allowed him back into the room but would not let him touch her. They fell asleep like that, and continued to sleep like that for the remainder of fall, then winter, then spring.

◆ ◆ ◆

Over the next few years, Joseph opened two more clinics and Anne took on several new clients. Joseph must have known why she could no longer be intimate with him but he did not ask her about it nor did she explain. Even in sleep he looked like he was in pain. She touched the burrows in his face. But even his pain did not change what she was feeling. Eventually he will find a lover, she thought to herself, like last time.

◆ ◆ ◆

As soon as he could again work the soil, Joseph planted more fruit trees. She watched him from the house, pruning, watering, and encouraging each one. There were now over one hundred of them—apple trees and peach trees, apricot and nectarine, cherry, date, and pomegranate.

The trees took turns flowering against the backdrop of the hill.

He is trying to seduce me, Anne thought to herself.

Each year, it would almost work.

It would start in the spring, when the cherry trees

blossomed. She would open her window and lie back on her bed, letting the scent envelop her. In the summer she would lie naked, mouth open, tasting the scents— lemon and orange, peach and pomegranate.

She knew that Joseph watched—and by the end of the summer, would consider being with him. But then the first frost would set in, she would again be looking at ice covered branches and remembering what had happened.

◆ ◆ ◆

He had asked her to be with him only once, at the end of his life. She knew he was embarrassed to have to ask her but she still said no.

"You're ill," she told him.

He kissed her hand instead.

She gave him his medicine.

◆ ◆ ◆

Joseph was gone now and she was alone in the house. Yesterday had been the first day of winter, the first winter without him, and she had looked out at his fruit trees. They stood against the hill-- bare, black and brittle. She shut the bedroom window.

Now she opened the envelope.

Inside was a photo of a dark-haired girl with green eyes and a blue sweater sitting at the foot of Gellért Hill. She sat down and took the photo out. Was it that girl again? She looked at it closer. No, it was not that girl again. It was herself as a young woman. Included in the envelope was a packet of fruit seeds. She spilled his seed into her hand then looked again at the photo. He had not been trying to seduce her. He had been trying to apologize. Each fruit tree he planted had been one more attempt at an apology.

She opened the backyard door.

All one hundred trees were coated in a thick layer of ice-- the branches, the bark, all the way down to the individual buds. Morning light shot through the ice, illuminating the trees, the hill, and every blade of grass; for these, too, were encased in ice.

Then the popping sound began. Ice breaking. But it was not coming from outside. It was happening on the inside.

"I'm sorry, Joseph. I'm sorry Joseph," she cried, the light in her face, kissing the back of her hand.

1015467321

Nancy Gunzberg had been in catering for twenty-one and a half years. It could have been twenty-two but she sprained her back in the middle of January while carrying a tray of assorted mini-quiches. Once her back healed, she was back as well, back to making wedding cold calls, Hanukah orders, mousaki and yelling at her staff.

"1015467321," she shouted from the back of her small office.

Two young women worked in the front of the large room processing orders. Both of them temps -- no health insurance, no contract, no job security, no benefits of any kind, each one just hoping to get through one more day so they could come back for another.

Customers had a copy of their catalogue and order form that they would fill out and fax in. Once received, the young women had to retype them into their computers using proper language—proper catering language. Set up time half an hour before the actual time listed by the customer. Six ounce versus eight ounce for the beverages. Too many cookies for that number of people. Outside the room versus inside.

Tables covered and skirted. Would pink linens have to special ordered? Lemon ice water comes in carafes not pitchers.

Becky, the newer temp of the two, jumped when she heard the numbers. She did not know *exactly* which part of Lincoln Park it was from, but she could tell from the first four digits that it was Lincoln Park -- the area she was responsible for billing. Her co-worker covered downtown Chicago. She ran and opened the second of the heavy drawers against the wall and began to look through the orders for that month. The small company had not yet computerized their billing system so much of their time was spent filing and re-filing orders. Invoicing had been turned in yesterday, so Becky assumed that she probably had made an error for March billing. Perhaps she had billed the wrong client's account, or perhaps she had left off some items that were supposed to have been billed, or perhaps the client was not to have been billed at all. She thought about all of these options and the hundred other combinations as she tried to keep her hands from trembling.

Her co-worker, Heather, did not look at her but continued to process her downtown orders.

"1015467321," Nancy yelled again from the back office, though her "back" office was only a few feet away from the girls and they were all basically in the same large room.

Becky flipped through the files faster. She knew she should probably just ask Nancy what the problem was, ask her why exactly she was yelling that number out, but she was trying to avoid doing so. 1015467319, 1015467320, 1015467322. Ugh! It skipped it. That was the one she was shouting about. Darnn it.

She probably wants to revise the order and use it for a different client. Oh God. What was she going to tell her? Maybe she had placed it in a different month's folder. She got to the last file. Nothing. And it looked like several invoices were missing in that month as well. She would have to ask Nancy.

She slowly walked back to Nancy's office, pausing a few times because she thought she would either faint or throw up. Maybe both? Could one do both? She got to the door.

"Hi Nancy. Sorry to interrupt you but I was wondering if you could please tell me what's wrong with invoice 1015467321?"

Nancy did not look up nor did she say anything. Becky knew she was breathing because she could see her large chest moving up and down to the rhythm of the two guppies kept in a punch bowl beside her. She was holding on to a piece of paper in front of her with dirty fingers. Her half-blonde half-black hair was disheveled and it looked like her moustache was growing back in.

Heather had told her over lunch yesterday that Nancy was in the mob.

"I don't believe you."

"Why not?"

"Her last name is German."

"That's the only reason you don't believe me?"

They both started laughing.

"1015467321," Nancy thundered as if Becky was still across the room.

"Yes, thank you for repeating that vital piece of information. Could you please tell me what's wrong with it?"

"Where the hell is it?"

Becky looked around. She hadn't meant to but she was nervous and she couldn't help it. Her eyes must have had some sort of involuntary muscle spasm and rolled around. Nancy's office was a wreck. Papers and receipts kept falling from her desk like November leaves. Half-eaten croissants and scones acted as paperweights. After all this time they might actually be weights. Stacks of books on management -- *Inspiring Your People* and *Lead by Example* were behind her, still wrapped in plastic. Figures, Becky thought. Then said, "Maybe it's in here."

Heather gasped.

It just came out. Oh God. Her mouth must have the same problem as her eyes. "Excuse me?" asked Nancy, now looking directly at her.

"It was just a suggestion that maybe it was accidentally left in here."

Nancy was quiet. Even her chest did not move. Becky was changing color, from her usual ivory to a burnt sienna to a sky blue to an ash gray and finally to white. The guppies took another lap across the bowl and so did her life. Not all of it, just a few key moments. Like the money she had squandered from her first real job. She wished she had managed it better. She wished someone would have taught her how. Maybe then she would've had something to live off of today. Or the conversation with her ex-boyfriend, the one that went something like, "Why don't you quit your job and come move in with me? Don't worry, I'll take care of you..."

"Get out of here," Nancy shouted. "And find it. I don't care if you have to lick the filing cabinet to do so."

Becky turned around and went back to the filing cabinet, passing Heather who was now on the phone. Becky opened the first drawer and began to look again.

The Renovation

She decided to put gold chunks in the mortar. Not real gold, the art store didn't carry real gold, but the cheaper stuff, the small rocks painted gold.

"Those are *real* gold," the stock boy had told her without her asking. "18K." He had opened a box next to her and was pulling out yarn balls in red, yellow and green.

What a delightful job, she thought to herself. She wished she too could spend the day pulling out yarn balls in red, yellow and green.

"Not on the inside though, right?"

"No, not on the inside. But who's going to check?"

She did not reply, but put the nuggets in her cart.

◆ ◆ ◆

Nicholas and Nora had been married for three years before purchasing their first home in Muncie, Indiana. Nicholas had been assigned a residency in radiology at Ball Memorial Hospital. Nora had been assigned a residency in cardiology.

Nora did not like medicine as much as Nicholas. Now thirty-four, she had spent most of her last ten years reading books that she was not interested in, taking classes in topics she was not interested in, getting a degree in something she was not interested in.

How ironic, she often thought when performing heart surgery, that she had such little connection to her own.

She had met Nicholas during one of her second-year rotations. He had the fundamental qualities she was looking for: smart, handsome, hard working, and like her, very insecure. The last quality, she figured, would be what kept them together. With both of them worrying if either of them would leave the other, the relationship would last forever.

"What are you wearing?" he had asked her, as she was about to leave for the art store.

"It's a turtleneck, Nicholas. Come on."

"It's too tight."

"No it isn't."

She looked at herself in the mirror. He stood next to her.

"Yes, it is," he said again. "Now go change. I don't want my wife getting stared at."

She went to the bedroom to change. When she came out, she noticed a red scarf hanging out of his coat pocket.

"Where did you get that?"

"What?" "That scarf."

"I bought it."

"When?"

"Last weekend when you were visiting your mother."

"You hate to shop. I don't believe you."

"I bought the stupid scarf last weekend."

"You just said you bought it when I was visiting my mother. I visited her two weekends ago not last weekend."

"I just got the weekends confused."

"Who bought it?"

"I did."

"I don't believe you."

"*I bought it, Nora!*"

They were now both in the kitchen.

"Fine," he said. And threw the scarf in the garbage.

"I thought you said you were going to change?"

"I did."

"To that?"

"It's in style."

"I can see your breasts."

"Of course you can see my breasts. I'm female."

"Go change."

"Who bought the scarf?"

"Go change."

"Who bought the scarf?"

His pager went off. He had to leave for the hospital. Nora left for the store.

◆ ◆ ◆

She held half a dozen nuggets in her hand. She was in South Dakota. No, she was not in South Dakota but she would have liked to have been. Unfortunately, Nicholas did not want to go to South Dakota, so she could not go either. They had agreed, when they had gotten married, that they would take all their vacations together. But when she looked at gold nuggets or fruit trees in plant stores from Costa Rica and Ecuador, she wished that she had not made the promise and could travel alone.

Last summer they had decided to renovate their house instead of taking a vacation. After two weeks, the repairs that needed to get done were completed. The house was fine. But they kept going.

Crack. Boom. Crack. Squeak. Crack. Boom.

Nicholas was now pulling up tile in the basement's bathroom to lay down tile that was half a shade lighter.

"Can I help you?" she asked.

"No," he yelled, without looking up. "Why don't you go work on the upstairs instead?"

There was no reason to work on the upstairs. The upstairs was fine. The downstairs was fine. The basement was fine. The whole house was fine. The previous owners had renovated the entire house two years ago. But winter was coming. Soon she would be in sweaters. If they did not renovate, what would there be left to talk about?

Boom. Bam. Boom. Splutz.

She had not told Nicholas her idea to put gold chunks around the fireplace. She was tired of renovating, which was now virtually all year long, without seeing a difference. The walls had been repainted white. The wood floors in the dining room had been re-stained the same color. The front porch had been demolished and rebuilt using the same floor plan. The study had been re-carpeted seven times using the same color and manufacturer. He had wanted to re-carpet an eighth time, which was why she had left for her mother's house.

This time, she thought, shaking her bag of rocks, there would be a noticeable difference.

She went to the garage to get some mortar and brought a ladder into the living room. Fortunately, Nicholas' pager went off and he rushed passed her, red scarf now wrapped twice around his throat.

She felt bad spreading the mortar on the fireplace's black marble, but the feeling went away once she set her first nugget. Sunlight hit rock, creating not just a physical reaction.

This must be what it feels like to strike gold, she thought, putting the mortar down to stare then celebrate.

After a while, she stopped working altogether to go lie down on the couch. She had been in surgery the night before but it was not that. She felt like she had been traveling.

◆ ◆ ◆

Nicholas put his keys down on the counter and walked into the living room. She had told him that she would be working on a living room project -- but they had agreed that she would be re-painting the walls, not *this*.

With morning light, the walls were exceptionally bright. Twinkle. The room twinkled. Gold nuggets were embedded in the wall every six inches. He walked up to the wall and touched one. There would be no way to take them out without damaging the walls.

"The fireplace!"

Gold nuggets were embedded in the marble and in the mantel.

He needed water.

He went into the kitchen. Light speckled his face.

Gold nuggets were embedded in all the kitchen walls.

He put down his glass. He took off his coat.

Gold nuggets were all over the house. Every single room. Gold nuggets. Gold nuggets. Embedded in the walls, on furniture, even inside closets and drawers.

The laundry room looked untouched. He went inside. No, even on the floor!

Up ahead, more on the ground. He followed the trail till he got outside. He was now standing in their driveway. Nora was almost done embedding all of this too. She was only one foot away from where their driveway met the open road. Her shoulders were bronzed. She was wearing a sleeveless shirt.

"They're not real on the inside," she said without looking up.

Andalusia

He walked her home at the end of their weekend together, crossing Harvard Bridge to get her there. It was Sunday night in the summer time: students and foreigners, tourists and businessmen crossed then re-crossed Charles River. The bridge smelled of pralines, vanilla, cologne and cognac. Sonya retraced her steps so she could again inhale vanilla.

Up ahead were three Andalusian street performers. Onar's favorite. He usually made her stop to listen to them and gave them all of his change. But this time he walked past them. They had gotten to know him, even knew him by name. The two bearded ones shouted out, "Onar," but he did not stop. He did not even look up till they were near the center of the river. For a few feet, now, it was just the two of them.

"I don't think we should see each other anymore," he said to her.

Sonya stopped walking and looked at him. The musicians were not that far behind and she could see them too. The bearded ones waved to her. Onar took her hand and walked her further out towards the center of the river.

146

"I don't see the point," he continued. "I just keep getting more and more attached to you and it's not ever going to work out."

"Work out? What does that really mean, Onar? Even if we were to get married there would be no guarantee it would work out."

"So you have the American mentality."

"Of what?"

"Divorce."

"No, I have the American mentality of possibility."

"You say things like that and it makes it all the harder to leave you."

"So why are you?"

"I don't have a choice."

"Yes you do. You've told me you can't marry me from the minute you met me."

"And I haven't changed my mind. I haven't lied to you."

"But I know you have feelings for me."

"It doesn't matter if I do or not."

"I can't take this anymore."

"Neither can I."

The music got louder, strumming the chords flamenco-style.

He took her hand again to move further down but she would not go this time.

"I like it here," she said and turned to face the river.

They did not say anything for a few minutes.

"I just think this is for the best," he said from behind her.

"You think? Well what do you feel?"

"I told you that it doesn't matter what I feel. I know the

statistics of these situations."

"What situation?"

"Interracial and interfaith marriages. They don't have a good survival rate."

She turned back to him.

"My parents did."

"Come on, Sonya. Most of them don't."

"You don't even know me. What makes me the angriest is that you don't even know me, and we have seen each other, what? Twice a week for the past three months?"

"I know you, Sonya."

"No, you don't! You're ending this prematurely!"

"I do know you. How many times does one need to look at *that*," pointing to the moon, "to know it is beautiful? How many times does one need to listen to *that* music to know it is beautiful?"

"My family comes from that region," she said.

"Which?"

"Andalusia."

He was quiet.

"I don't know why you even want to be with me, Sonya. You could have anyone. You could have some tall, wealthy, handsome American guy who will give you everything you want. Not some poor student from Bangladesh who can't commit to you."

"I'm not going to degrade what we have and what I feel by listing the ten things I love about you."

She turned back to the river.

"Only ten?"

She didn't laugh. Normally, she would have.

"I'm going to miss you," he said.

"You're still going to do it?" she asked, turning back around.

He became very stern again.

"It's not my choice."

"It is always your choice."

"My family wants me to marry a Bengali woman who is Muslim. I want her to be able to speak Bengali to my mother."

"I thought your mother was a physician."

"She is."

"And she speaks English?"

"She does."

"Don't lie to me. It's obvious that this is a lie. You just don't like me. It's not about my race or religion. You just don't want to be with *me*."

"I thought you were intelligent."

"I am intelligent but I'm not perfect."

"Who is? We're all human."

"I think you're inhuman in your ability to give up our connection. If you truly do care about me, then it is masochistic to do this. You're going against your nature."

"They're just feelings, Sonya. They don't matter. What matters is what is important to my family."

"If your family loved you, they would want you to be happy."

"If I loved them, I would want them to be happy. And I do love them."

"Your responsibility should be to yourself."

"I am my family. There is no 'I'."

"My family would prefer that I marry a Christian, but whoever I loved, they would love him too."

A couple walked by holding hands. She began to cry.

"Aren't you going to say goodbye to me?" he said.

"No. I don't agree with what you're doing. I'm not going to acknowledge it."

"Then I will have to say it for the both of us."

She did not reply. She wanted to turn again and face the river but she forced herself to face him.

"I know we have a connection, Sonya. I don't want you to ever look back at this and say to yourself that you imagined it. Because you didn't."

Now he too was crying.

He tried to kiss her but she would not let him. She did not see what happened next. She did not look at the river but neither could she look up. Her eyes were too full of tears and the music was in her ears and all she could feel was sadness. When she did look up, the music had stopped and he was gone. She retraced their steps to see if perhaps he had stopped back by the musicians but they too were gone. And then she thought to herself that she had imagined it all, until she remembered what he had told her.

Building the Brooklyn Bridge

I.

Her grandfather had come from Italy, from Mola di Bari (near the heel of the boot) and had gotten a job as a mason, helping to build the Brooklyn Bridge on the Brooklyn side. If his English had been better, he could have helped design it, for he was just as good at math and physics as he was with cement.

Antoinette, like her grandfather, had a great love for science—especially engineering. Perhaps if there had been sons in the family her grandfather would not have encouraged her. But she was the only grandchild, the only child altogether, for both her parents had died on the boat to America. Her grandfather had raised her himself.

◆ ◆ ◆

By late afternoon, Antoinette would be finished with the reading her grandfather had assigned and would be headed to the East River. At the end of Fulton Street, horsecars would be making their turnaround by the ferry house. At the start of the river, Fulton Ferry, South Ferry, and Wall Street Ferry would be pulling in or heading out. Further out on the water, steamers, yachts, clipper ships, and schooners would be crisscrossing the river heading to New York or coming back. She watched them-- toy boats from a distance-- till they arrived in the harbor, crossing the river and coming back, crossing the river and coming back more times than the sea gulls overhead.

Three puffs from the chimney of one of the largest distilleries. The Wall Street ferry had just landed. Shop girls and businessmen, day laborers and butchers, storekeepers and bank tellers rushed off the boat, more men and women got on. The South Ferry landed. Tailors and fishermen, priests and silversmiths got on. Five puffs from another distillery and two factories. More people got off.

There used to be a day when she could recognize many of the men and women who got on and off the ferries-- even knew some of their names. Steve with the charcoal bang-up worked in diamonds. Jerry with the black browler worked at a clothing store. Anne with the turban and peach-colored gigot sleeves was in love with Steve but married to Jerry. Antoinette did not see any of them now. Brooklyn and New York were growing. Some of the smoke cleared with the five o'clock breeze. There were many more people now who also wanted to cross the river.

She pulled out a licorice from her pantaloons and moved further down the waterfront --past the distilleries, factories, and warehouses that made Brooklyn so enticing-- and eventually sat down on the edge of the dock. Fortunately, Grandfather did not make her wear dresses. She untucked her blouse and looked up at the men.

The men were on land close to the river building the first caisson—a giant, bottomless, wooden box, more than half the size of the new Saint Cathedral. Soon the caisson would be filled with compressed air and slowly sent to the bottom of the river by building up layers of stone on its roof. Later, a second caisson would be built on the New York side. On top of these two caissons, the towers would be built, and from these towers the bridge would stretch across the East River.

"Over here," her grandfather suddenly yelled, thrashing his arms around. "More stone over here!"

Her grandfather was on top of the box with dozens of other men. As they continued to add weight, the box slowly sank.

Though much younger than her grandfather, the men looked small in comparison to him. He was 6'3" and she knew part of it had to do with his size, but most of it had to do with his personality. Some, when unfamiliar with a country and its language, might have tried to be modest. Or at the least, quiet. Vulnerability made her grandfather louder, more aggressive and more competitive.

"Aren't you ashamed?" her girl friend, Kathleen, had once asked her, after witnessing one of her grandfather's explosions.

"Of what?" she replied.

They had been waiting on her grandfather outside the bank and could still hear him cursing out the teller.

"It's not his fault he's smarter and stronger than all of them," Antoinette continued.

Some of the men listened to him and attached more stone to the pulley. Others left to work on a different section of the box.

Then air pressure was being used to pump out sand. The rest of the men stepped away.

Now as she watched him work alone, with the sun setting behind him, it was as if he was the only one building the great bridge.

◆ ◆ ◆

They lived close to the site, in a tenement house south of Navy Yard. Most of the residents in the building were Irish, though occasionally an Italian family would move in.

"Watch out," he yelled when they got home-- opening and closing cupboards, doors, and windows. She sat in the corner of the kitchen and watched him swinging wood this time, instead of iron. She got up to start the dishes.

"No dishes. I told you. No dishes, no cooking, no cleaning. Only study."

"But Grandfather, engineering schools do not want females."

"You are not female."

A knock on the door. Florella, the young Italian woman from down the hall. Grandfather told her Florella what housework needed to be done, then followed Antoinette into her side of their only other room.

"Mathematics," he said to her in English. She took her book and went over her solutions with him.

"Excellent. Now physics."

◆ ◆ ◆

He studied with her almost every night. He did not use Italian when he spoke to her. Only English.

"We are in America now and I want you to speak like America."

He turned the page of her textbook and studied the next problem. She studied his hair.

Though over sixty, her grandfather still had all his hair which raced, at varying speeds, like English ponies. Some of it came to his shoulders, some of it came out no further than a toothpick, some stayed behind his ears. Despite the different lengths, the color was the same all over— black. Her own hair was light brown but her grandfather said that she was only thirteen and it would darken as she got older. She hoped so. She also wanted to have hair like a crow and to be as wild and frightening as one.

◆ ◆ ◆

One day after school, she did not find her grandfather at the river, but in bed.

"Compression sickness," he told her. His skin was gray and he was holding his stomach and he couldn't stop shaking even when he was speaking to her. The worst sign, however, was his hair that was now thin, dull, and matted. She was not sure what to do. She had never seen her grandfather so sick before.

"Help me with my hair," he said.

She looked at him.

"My hair," he said louder. "The dye is under the wash stand."

She had not realized that he colored his hair.

She went to the corner of the room and found the dye, pulled out a tin tub and a pitcher and heated some water on the stove. When the water was done, her grandfather climbed down from the bed, turned around, and leaned back over the tub.

"Don't forget to shampoo first," he said lifting the back of his hair as she prepared the mixture. She looked up. There, underneath, was the real color of his hair. White. White as a lily. White as a popcorn ball. White as coleslaw. White as a tea cake. White as a beaten biscuit before it was beaten. White as... white as all the things she could not imagine her grandfather being and did not want him to be. Surprised, she began trembling, and spilled water on him. His hair was half wet now and half white, clinging to his face like a splattered sea gull. He did not look like a crow anymore. He looked like an old man.

"It's not contagious," he said to her, taking the pitcher back.

II.

Anthony's grandmother had come from Italy, from Reggio di Calabria (near the toe of the boot) and had gotten a job as a dancer, dancing for the men who were building the New York side of the Brooklyn Bridge. If her English had been better, she could have helped design it, for she was just as good at math and physics as she was with her legs.

Anthony, unlike his grandmother, had a great love for dancing and often thought how wonderful it would be to dance across the new bridge. Both towers had now been built and a footbridge had been put in place. But his grandmother would not let him. Perhaps if more boys had been born into the family she would have let him pursue his own interests. But he was the only boy as well as the only child. His parents had not liked America and returned to Italy, abandoning his grandmother and him at the loading dock.

"É venuto come lei non me ha mai lasciato la guarda balla?" he asked his grandmother as he began to make dinner. They had a room now at a boarding house between Broadway and Hudson and were no longer living on the streets.

"In English, Anthony. English."

"How come you never let me watch you dance?" he repeated as he rubbed down a chicken.

"And no cooking. I don't want you to cook. Do your homework. I'll check on you when I am done."

In a few minutes she came into his room, her hands scented with thyme and shiny with oil. She wiped them on her breeches. Ever since coming to America, he had yet to see her in makeup, jewelry, or a dress. He had yet to see her looking feminine at all-- she kept her oval face plain and her hair tightly braided in small buns all around her head. Looking at them reminded him of anthills or black nuts. Yes, she was like a nut tree. Strong and productive.

"This one is wrong," she said to him in Italian. "Have you learned vectors yet?"

"No," he replied without looking up.

"In English, Anthony, in English."

"No is also 'no' in English."

"But you say it with an Italian accent."

"I *am* Italian."

"No, Anthony. Not anymore. You are American now and must speak like one. No accent. Not even a little one. You will not do well in this country until you learn English -- perfectly. This country does not tolerate weakness."

◆ ◆ ◆

A bridge over the East River joining New York and Brooklyn had been debated for a long time in bars, in shops and in the papers.

"New York and Brooklyn, unite!" declared Congressman Demass Barnes in the New York *Tribune*.

"The ice gorges will be the death of us," announced a Brooklyn barber in the Brooklyn *Eagle*.

But nothing was built.

The main problem was the East River—not a river at all, but a tidal strait, and one of the country's most dangerous. Fog, gorges, rain, and snow delayed and complicated the liquid path of New Jersey schooners carrying coal, Connecticut sloops carrying brick, and the Norwegian pennants with mainstops more than one hundred feet above their decks

"A great arch is needed," seven Brooklyn boys hollered, in between formation. Every Saturday, outside the Brooklyn Gas Company, five of the boys would form a bridge and two would impersonate schooners till one boy broke an ankle and another joined the navy.

They were building that great arch now.

The New York caisson had been successfully sunk, the granite towers constructed, the footbridge in place. They were now beginning to work on the four steel cables, two outer and two inner, which would go across the great bridge. Everyone was excited because they would be made of steel instead of iron wire as had always been done. There was not yet a structure in New York or in any other city built entirely of steel. The bridge would soon be not just a bridge, but a symbol for the country.

Anthony would take the sidewalk entrance on Park Row, just across from City Hall Park and sit down on the grass or snow (depending on the season) and watch the bridge's development. His grandmother would usually be there too. She had asked the foreman a few months ago if she could help build the bridge, but he had said no. No ladies allowed. But he could not stop her from watching. And she did, getting there early in the morning and leaving by late afternoon to prepare for her show.

A few weeks later, the foreman quit and a new one joined the crew. This one would not hire her either-- but he did allow her to help out.

Now, when Anthony visited, his grandmother would be working with the crew. They were working on the cables and wiring. Grandmother sat on the ground near the water, holding some of the pieces. She had pants on like the other men, a shirt and coat too. She was thin and sinewy, like the metal twine she was twisting. Just like at home, she wore no makeup here and her black hair would be braided even more tightly all over her small head, bringing more attention to her big, black eyes and small mouth.

"Spider," the new foreman told her. "You look like a spider weaving your web."

"Spider," they began to call her. "Hold this spot right here."

"Spider. Come measure this cable."

"Spider. Get us some water."

Better spider than darling, she thought, and she did what they asked and did her work well, hoping that one day they would pay her and forget she was female altogether.

"Aren't you ashamed?" asked his friend Nelson who had come to see the bridge with Anthony after work one day.

"Of what?" Anthony replied.

"Your grandmother."

"Why should I be? It's not her fault that she has a man's ambition."

She was now near the center of the bridge, with the steeples of Brooklyn's churches and distilleries behind her, and New York's beggars, billionaires and buildings in front of her. It was late afternoon. All along the four main cables, heavy, white wire shot down to the bridge floor in patient, vertical stripes. Crisscrossing the harp strings was round two of wiring-- diagonal wiring that radiated from the top of the tower like metallic sunrays. His grandmother adjusted the wiring-- looking like not so much like a spider but a musician tuning his autoharp. He imagined he could hear the music and turned a slow pirouette.

◆ ◆ ◆

A few weeks later Anthony came home from school instead of going straight to the park. He had bought some chocolate for his grandmother at *Eddies* near Trinity Church. He wanted to thank her for helping him with last night's homework. All of his—or rather her-- answers had been right. He put the chocolate on ice and was about to make himself some lemonade.

Music. He heard music coming from her bedroom

"She's dancing," he exclaimed. "Finally, I will see Grandmother dancing."

But when he looked in, Grandmother was not dancing. She was --

Screams. He started screaming. Then he started crying.

Two men came out of the room and left.

"Stop crying," she said to him, pulling the bed sheet around herself. "Stop crying. Only women cry."

He looked at her but she was not crying. Though her head was down he could see she had makeup on—violet eyes and darkened lashes. And her hair-- her hair was unbraided. The nuts had cracked open. He had never seen it down before. He had never seen her looking.... so female before.

"Don't worry," she said. "It's not contagious." Pulling her hair back up.

The Bald Lover

Suzanne was gone for the night, out with one of the married men she liked to date -- her favorite -- an old Japanese man who knew the color of ice. He had been with Suzanne as she said goodbye to Matthew and Priya. He was taking her ice skating at Rockefeller Center, Suzanne told them both, and she would not be home tonight. The Japanese man did not smile when she said this. He said nothing at all but turned around and walked her to his car.

"Perhaps he is tired of ice," Matthew said to Priya.

"How can she do that?" Priya said as the car pulled away. "She's thirty. He's sixty -- and married." She quickly added, "But who am I to judge?" before Matthew could respond. She put her book back on the shelf then walked back to Matthew's room and lied down on the bed.

◆ ◆ ◆

She had been intimate with Matthew several times in the few months that she had known him, but always with her hairpiece on.

"Not yet," she had said to him each time he touched it.

"But I want to see what you look like."

"This is what I look like."

"You know what I mean. Without your -- "

"Hairpiece on?"

He kissed her neck.

"Maybe later," she said. "Maybe next time Suzanne doesn't spend the night."

But Suzanne had continued to bring the married men home with her. Priya could hear them from Matthew's room even though Suzanne tried to cover up the noise with her singing.

"She's gone now."

"I know." Matthew had joined her on the bed. He was lying next to her, his leg across hers. His cheek on her chest.

She touched his hair.

Her mother did not know that she was dating Matthew. She would have been half-pleased. He was a scientist. He was from an upper middle-class family. He was 30. He had never been married. He was, however, white. Ideally her parents wanted her to marry someone who was not only Indian but also Jubali -- from her same village in southern India. But there were not many Jubali men on the planet -- 200,000 maybe and only a fraction eligible -- which is perhaps why her mother had been so troubled by her hair condition.

"Make it grow," her mother had told Priya's grandmother. But none of her grandmother's remedies had worked.

"Make it grow," she had said to the American doctor when Priya was fifteen and they had moved to the States.

"We don't know what's causing it."

"Make it grow," she had said to her husband.

"I'm a dentist, Anjeela, not a beautician. Leave the girl alone. I'm bald and you married me."

Priya laughed.

"It's bad enough that she is dark-skinned," she snapped back. Then she returned to vacuuming.

"It is bad enough that she is dark-skinned," Priya repeated to herself in darkness.

Matthew touched her hair again.

"Not yet," she whispered, and he put his head back on her chest.

◆ ◆ ◆

Her mother began to press her to marry when she turned eighteen. Priya knew why. With her dark skin and hair problem, her age would be her biggest asset in an arranged marriage.

"He likes your picture."

"I don't care. He's forty-two and divorced. I don't want to marry someone that much older than me and with children."

Her mother stopped chopping onions and looked at her.

"You do not have the looks to be so picky. You should feel lucky that this man is even considering you."

"I don't feel lucky."

"Well then maybe you should think about your family. Do you know how much you are hurting your family by not being married? Did you know that coming to your wedding was your dead grandmother's only wish?"

Priya stared at the onions, now frying in olive oil and cumin.

The phone rang. Her mother went to answer it. Priya left the room.

♦ ♦ ♦

Her mother had been married at seventeen and had told Priya that she had not been ready. But their horoscopes had matched perfectly -- so perfectly that she may never again have that kind of luck.

They had, in fact, been a good match. Her husband was kind. He did treat her well and she did grow to love him. But still, she had not been ready. And she had wished that luck could have been postponed.

Priya thought about her mother as she sat in her bedroom upstairs and the smell of cumin changed to ginger. What had happened to her memory?

I will buy myself luck, she decided. *I will make my own money. And with my daughter -- I will remember my own memories.*

♦ ♦ ♦

By the end of the year, her parents agreed to let her leave Minnesota to go to a private college on the East Coast. She had not had many suitors and her parents decided that if she could not get married, she might as well get educated. She would have to support herself somehow.

A part of her was now glad that she was not beautiful, she thought, as she packed her bags for college. She knew what happened to the beautiful ones. The ones like Tahera -- tall and slender, white as a Caucasian.

As the water level of their village rose after rain, fifteen year old Tahera used to take out her sketch book and draft aqueducts that would have made the Romans proud. *What a terrific engineer Tahera would make*, Priya thought, looking over her shoulder. But within two years, Tahera was married to a very rich man who could have been close to three hundred pounds and was hardly interested in Tahera's aqueducts.

Priya had heard about Tahera from a family friend just the other week. A fourth child on the way and rumors that her husband was cheating.

She would think about Tahera whenever it rained. *All of that wasted potential*, she thought again now as she watched the water come down outside her window. And she imagined what the world would be like if the Taheras of the world could be allowed to develop as people. The cities we could design, the medical discoveries we could make, the problems we could solve. It was 2002 and yet most of the women she knew would still face a world of washing machines and dinner parties. Better conditions -- a washing machine instead of a river, a condo instead of a Bhunga -- but the same limitations.

It was women who too often would hurt each other, she continued thinking. She was now walking through Chinatown in New York with her mother who was visiting for the week. She wanted to express these things to her but couldn't. She could hardly express much of anything to her parents—especially her mother.

She had tried to tell her mother when she was fourteen and they were still in India that she did not want to get married. Not like this. Not under these conditions. Perhaps she would marry at some point, but she would marry the right person for her. And she wanted her life to be about more than just marriage. She wanted the right to develop as a human being.

Her grandparents had been alive then and they were living together with them in that old house.

"I don't want to get married," she had begun. "Not for a long time anyway."

Her mother had been on the floor looking through her wedding album. She had looked up. Eyes darkening. Hands up in the air that then began to come down on her as well as other objects her mother grabbed. She hit her with the photos. She hit her with the album. She hit her with the pan that they had just used to heat up water. Some of the water had burned her skin, darkening her skin in those spots. She looked at the blisters forming as her mother continued to scream at her. *Like tumors*, she thought; *I wonder if they will also form on my head*, for some of the water had scorched her scalp as well. They did not form on her head, but the next day, her hair began to fall out.

It was late now. Two, maybe three in the morning. Matthew had fallen asleep hours ago. She checked to make sure before taking her hairpiece off. The front door opened. Suzanne was home. She was already singing and they had not even reached her room.

The Perfume Maker

He came from the town of Grasse in the south of France.
He could not say born because he did not know where he had
been born. Both his parents had been Spanish peddlers and his
mother had given birth to him in the back of their wagon somewhere along the French Riviera. They had stopped in Grasse
a few days later only to get some bread and cheese. Their stay
turned out to be longer than expected, for his mother fell ill
with the Spanish influenza and died by the end of the month.

His father had been surprised at his wife's death. The
Spanish influenza was supposed to have ended almost ten
years ago. Nevertheless, he buried his wife in a field of
daffodils, gave up peddling and got a job as a factory worker
in Grasse where flowers were processed for their essential
oil. As for the boy-- he could not afford to hire a nanny for
the child so he would lay him in fields of violets, carnations
or wild lavender before he went into work then pick him up
a few hours later after his shift had ended. Within a week, his
baby took on the scents of the flower fields, sometimes even
the coloring.

When the boy got older, the father built a small house for them on a hill behind the daffodil field where he had buried his wife. Now it was only he that would come home every day smelling of a different flower. Some days it would be lily of the valley. Some days it would be rose. Some days it would be honeysuckle. Some days it would be hyacinth. The scent of rose, lily of the valley or hyacinth enhanced his father's black hair, blue eyes and stature. To the boy, his father was not only very beautiful but also as tall and strong as the oak tree in front of their kitchen window.

In the evenings, he would stare at the tree as he awaited his father's return from the factory. Usually that meant staying up till three or four in the morning, but the boy did not mind. If he did not stay up to see him, he would hardly see him at all. So while he waited, he admired the oak tree against the moon and imagined that their tree was the Chapel-Oak of Allouville-Bellefosse— one of the oldest and largest trees in France. Each year thousands of people visited the famous oak which was more a religious monument and object of pilgrimage than a tree. Their oak tree did not get nearly as many visitors—just his father and occasionally red poppies.

One spring night he stayed up till four then five in the morning yet his father still did not arrive. Finally at dawn, the doorknob wiggled, the door pushed open and his father walked in. May's sun was just beginning to rise behind him, highlighting the silver stripes of his factory uniform and the silver steaks in his otherwise black hair. The boy jumped into his arms and hugged his father who was now enveloped in morning light. The boy blinked then inhaled. His father was wearing a new scent. A scent he had never smelled before. It was light, delicate yet lush.

"What is it, Father?"

"French jasmine," his father responded.

The boy inhaled again, taking in a deep breath of the velvety soft scent. By the time he had exhaled, he had decided. He was going to become a perfume maker.

◆ ◆ ◆

Most of the boys that began the formal training course at Joubert Perfumery School were between the ages of 23-27. At 13, the boy was the youngest in his class, and in fact, in the history of the region.

They had admitted him one week after taking his aptitude test. In the first test he was asked to identify different odors that were presented on smelling blotters. The smells ranged from peanuts and leather to nutmeg and green apples. He was so talented that he got not only the smells right, but he could also tell what had been on the hand of the person who had handled the smelling blotter.

"Yogurt," he had said to the tester, a fifth generation Joubert and man of at least seventy who had perfumed his white hair so often with rose water that it was now a deep shade of pink. "Sprinkled with cashews and raisins."

"That's not what is on the blotter," the pink-haired man replied. "But it is what I had for breakfast."

Next the boy was given the triangle test. He was presented,

in random order, with three blotters of which two were identical and the third slightly different.

"Caramel, caramel and brown sugar," said the boy.

"Very good," said the tester. "Though that is what had been on the blotters yesterday."

The old man paused before giving him the next test.

"Marcel," he said to his assistant. "Vite! Donnez-moi quelques nouveaux buvards sentants!"

The assistant came back with blotters that had never been used before. In fact, they had been made from three types of wood that very day. The assistant dipped them into small bottles of scent and handed them to the boy.

"Oak, maple and cherry wood," he said to the tester. "The scents on top, however, are lemon, lemon and lime."

"Amazing," said the tester. "Vous êtes magnifique!"

♦ ♦ ♦

The following afternoon was the last part of the test. The old trainer had not slept well because he had been thinking about it. Yes, the boy definitely had the physiological prerequisites for a career in perfumery, but there was more to a successful career than that. He would have to spend many hours, many years training, much of it by himself. He would encounter frequent disappointments and much frustration as little of his work was selected and rewarded. There was only one way to counter these difficulties. He would have to have joy—joy for the sake of creating.

"Marcel," he said to his assistant. "Vite! Donnez-moi un parfum spécial pour le garçon."

The assistant came back with a scented blotter and presented it to the boy. The boy took the blotter and inhaled. The trainer watched the boy's face as he did so.

His eyes had been closed as he inhaled but they now, slowly opened. In his mind, he could again see the start of the sunrise he had experienced the day his father had returned home from the factory. He could feel himself again, in the arms of his father, holding him, his face close to his warm neck and then the scent, the same scent that he smelled now. The warm, delicate, lush scent of-

"French jasmine," he said out loud.

"Correct," he said to the boy. "He has the joy," the trainer said to himself. "He has the joy," he shouted out loud, hugging the boy, then his assistant, leaving both slightly pink and smelling of rose water.

◆ ◆ ◆

Because the boy was at a much higher level of olfactory development than the rest of the students, after one week, he was pulled from class and put on a rigid program of self-training. He was assigned to a smelling cabin behind the main building of the perfumery school made entirely of glass— except for a single silver desk and chair and several rows of laboratory-like shelves that ran all around the one-room cabin. Once an hour, deodorized air kept at a constant temperature would be pumped into the room.

The boy's first assignment was to develop a foundation in "notes" as the old man called them-- the ingredients of a perfume.

"Perfume," the trainer explained, "Is not just a random combination of pleasant materials. Perfume has a well-defined structure. Each element plays its role in creating the overall effect. In fact, perfume has much in common with music. The first part is the top or head note which introduces the theme, then disappears. Next you have the middle note, the heart of the perfume. It must be made of material that will set the theme of the fragrance for hours. Finally, you have the bottom note which gives the perfume depth, and like a resonating chord, echoes on the skin for a day or two."

He paused for a moment and looked around the room.

"But before one can begin to compose, one must learn his notes."

Rows and rows of glass bottles lined the shelves of the glass cabin. In each of them was a note. Some were pleasant, many were not. The boy was required to learn all of them, his instructor had said before exiting the cabin. The boy pulled his chair up to his desk and began with the first one. One after another, he put the blotter to his nose and formed an association. This note smells like spruce bark. This note smells like candle wax. This note smells like chocolate cake batter. In this manner, he quickly learned fifty of them. Some, like cinnamon bark, oakmoss, lavender, and lemongrass were immediately recognizable. For notes like labdanum extract, petitgrain paraguay and vetyver bourbon, association helped him remember them.

Between notes, he jotted down descriptive comments and impressions, comparisons and curiosities. Between smelling

175

sessions, he went outside, inhaled, then turned around and began again.

♦ ♦ ♦

In a few weeks he had mastered the hundreds of pleasant and unpleasant smells from the bottles lining the laboratory shelves. In another few weeks, he had mastered the most important floral accords. He left his cabin to tell his trainer.

The trainer was not in his office so the boy began to search the grounds. In an hour he had located the pink-haired man. He was on the other side of the main building holding a set of keys.

"Come with me," the trainer said to him. The boy followed the old man to the back of the main building then through a small doorway that went underground. Within a few minutes, they had reached what looked like a wine cellar. It was cold and dark in the stonewalled room. The old man lit a candle. The boy looked around. More metal shelving and hundreds of metal flasks much larger than the ones that he had been working with surrounded them.

"The flasks you see around you do not contain wine, but perfume. Over 2,000 different kinds archived from around the world. Most of the leading perfume companies have committed to giving us 16 ounces of every new perfume they create. In addition to the new perfume we get each season, we have old and rare perfumes as well." He got a ladder and brought down a dull, metal flask. Using one of the keys from his key ring, he opened the flask then handed it to the boy.

"Rosemary, sage, thyme, citrus and lavender oil in an alcohol base," said the boy, after smelling the blotter.

"Very good," said the old man. "It's a 14th century perfume called Eau de La Reine de Hongrie or Hungary Water, commissioned by Queen Elizabeth of Hungary. As you can smell, one does not need lots of material to create a great fragrance. Even just a few notes in the right combination can work."

He retrieved another flask.

The boy smelled the blotter.

"Crisp and lemony."

"Eau de Cologne de Napoléon I à Saint-Hélène," said the old man. "Napoleon loved to smell good even during battle."

The old man gathered several more flasks in a basket and handed it to the boy.

"These are some of the greatest perfumes of all time. Take these back to the cabin. Your next assignment is to deconstruct their formulas then recreate the fragrances. You will learn the importance of balancing simplicity and complexity in composition as well as beauty and subtlety with strength and staying power. A great perfume is not only aesthetically successful, it is also well-made."

The boy thanked his trainer then headed back to his cabin.

◆ ◆ ◆

Within a week the boy had deconstructed three of the most recent, great perfumes—Shalimar, Chanel No. 5 and Mitsouko. Every hour, cool, deodorized air would pump into the cabin and push out a famous fragrance through the glass chimney. Out puffed Shalimar. Out puffed Chanel No. 5. Out puffed Mitsouko. The following week, more beautiful fragrances were squeezed into the sky-- L'Heure Bleu and Arpège.

By the end of the month, the boy had gone in descending order, deconstructing and recreating the greatest perfumes in history. On Friday he took his morning break wearing Hungary Water. On Saturday he smelled like Napoleon in battle and on Sunday he left his glass cabin to find his trainer, smelling of frankincense and myrrh.

He found his trainer in a lavender field about two kilometers from the main building. The boy waited till his trainer had stopped picking flowers then handed him the basket. It was filled with glass bottles along with the original metal flasks. The trainer compared the perfumes. One after another matched perfectly. The trainer kissed the boy on the head and handed him a bouquet of lavender.

"Will you be giving me more perfumes to match?" asked the boy.

"No," replied his trainer. "You're now familiar with all the notes we have in stock. It's time for you to become intimate with the thousands of notes out there."

"Where?" asked the boy.

"There," said the trainer, lifting his eyes to the horizon.

◆ ◆ ◆

Before sunrise, the boy stepped out of his glass cabin into the midsummer night. He got down on his knees and smelled the wet grass. Then he stood up and smelled the bark of the cherry trees next to his cabin. It began to rain and he caught some of it in his hands and smelled that too. He went into the woods and came upon a fallen deer and smelled fresh musk for the first time. He continued walking through the woods smelling dogwood, orange blossom, truffles and blackberries.

He walked out of the woods and across France to the Middle East, smelling cuttlefish powder from Saudi Arabia, balsam from Egypt and the cedar trees of Lebanon. Later he smelled almonds from Syria, pomegranates from Turkey and wild plums from Tunisia.

He crossed the ocean and smelled the *Angraecum sesquipedale* orchid of Madagascar, lettuce coral of the Phoenix Islands and Fiji's Great Astrolabe Reef. He smelled the spreading paulownia tree of Shijiawan in east central China and the snow peak east of Qoriwayrachina, a previously unknown Inca settlement. He smelled rye from Finland, torch ginger from Indonesia and the venom of the south Sahara Gaboon viper.

When he returned to the perfumery school, he was no longer a boy but a young man. His trainer was now a very old man. He found him in a field of carnations. At first, the young man did not recognize him because he no longer had pink hair. He no longer had hair at all.

"I've smelled the world," he told the old man. "I'm ready to create my own perfume."

"Have you dreamt your perfume?" asked the trainer, bending back down to gather more carnations.

"What do you mean?"

"In your dreams, have you dreamt your perfume?"

"No," the young man replied. "I have not dreamt my perfume."

The old man stood up.

"The greatest perfumes of the world have been imagined before they have been created. They are someone's vision of beauty, of history, of a promise, of hope. Just like a painting, a poem or a song—a perfume too must evoke an emotion, a perspective, an observation, a memory. Otherwise, perfume would become just a chemical composition and you would have to ask humanity to wear detergent, not art."

The young man returned to his glass cabin and sat down by his rusted metal desk. He could no longer see the carnation field but he remembered it, just like he now remembered all the things he had seen and smelled over the past ten years. He looked around at the glass bottles, each one properly identified. Then he looked out again through the other side of the cabin. He used to be able to see his father's factory from here. His father's factory. Oh, his poor father. Look how it had all changed. He approached the glass. The once stately brick building was now disheveled and crumbling. Several of the hand crafted windows were shattered. Men still went in and out of the factory but their uniforms were tattered, dirty, their faces forlorn. One of them looked like his father.

"Father!" he shouted as he left his glass cabin to hail down the worker.

During the years that the boy had been in school then

smelling the world, his father had continued to work at the perfume factory. Between smelling blotters, the boy looked forward to the day when his father's factory would produce the perfume he had created and he would make his hardworking father chief of operations.

He had been in touch with his father during the past ten years of his travels, but the letters had been one sided since he never stayed in any one place long enough to receive his post. What his father would have written is that his flower factory had changed. Management had changed their extraction method from enfleurage to chemical extraction. The factory had not been well-ventilated. He had been inhaling noxious fumes for the past ten years.

The worker whom the young man had been yelling at was not his father. But he did tell him where his father was. When the young man made it back to his childhood home, his father was sitting on the stone steps, fatigued and light green.

"You're ill," he said to him, putting his arms around him.

His father had changed over the years as much as the oak tree had next to their house. Or perhaps it was because the boy was older. He had been mistaken about the oak tree. It was not an oak tree but a shrub, not much higher than his chest and he was not a tall man. The boy put his face close to his father's. His father no longer smelled of French jasmine. Once his factory had switched from enfleurage to chemical extraction they had decided to stop processing the expensive flower. Now his father smelled like dirt, sweat and ammonia. He took his face away from his father's and looked at him. Without the fragrance of French flowers, his father was not beautiful but average. His father was an average man.

◆ ◆ ◆

The young man cried for weeks till his glass cabin fogged up like a rain forest. The air was thick and wet with tears and it took the old trainer a long time to find the young man. He had fallen asleep under the rusted metal table.

The old man had just laid his hands on him when the young man awoken.

"I have dreamt my perfume," he said.

The fog began to clear out.

The next day was the beginning of May and the French jasmine fields were being harvested. The young man helped. He went out into the lush fields of the delicate white flowers and gathered them by the armful. He gathered flowers all day, and the next and the next till he had enough to make his perfume.

"Now I need my bottom note."

He walked to the woods behind the perfumery school till he found an oak tree and gathered some oakmoss. Then he headed to the factory where his father had worked and scraped metal from one of the machines.

"Now I need a top note."

He waited till morning when the sun was out, and squashed a morning beam into the crystal bottle.

Together, the notes created the scent of the father he had remembered, the father he had imagined.

"It's called 'Père,'" he told his old trainer, handing him the bottle.

The morning beam ran under the old man's nose then flew out, leaving the heart of freshly harvested French jasmine and the earthy, vibrant smell of oakmoss deepened by the chord of silver metal.

"What do you think?"

The old man smiled then closed the bottle.

"You have created a great perfume."

DINA RABADI was born in Ajloun, Jordan in 1974 to a Jordanian father and a Czech mother. Dina and her family immigrated to the United States in 1978. A graduate of Smith College, she has been published in over twenty periodicals including The *Boston Globe*, *The Chicago Tribune*, *The Los Angeles Times*, and *Fiction*. Rabadi is the recipient of grants and awards from the Illinois Arts Council, the Vogelstein Foundation and a writing residency from the Sitka Center for Art and Ecology in Oregon.

www.ingramcontent.com/pod-product-compliance
Lightning Source LLC
Chambersburg PA
CBHW060156130626
46556CB00006B/2669